A Handful Of Beginnings

Abhiram Ravikumar

WRITERS' READERS
AN IMPRINT OF BOOKSTHAKAM

Published by Booksthakam, India

info@booksthakam.com

www.booksthakam.com

A Handful of Beginnings

A Booksthakam Book/ published by arrangement with the author

ISBN: 978-93-94378-74-2

Typeset and Cover Design by Cogitabund LLP

Printed and bounded in India by Manipal Technologies Limited

FSC www.fsc.org MIX Paper | Supporting responsible forestry FSC® C043100

Table of Contents

To my Parents and my Brother.

Acknowledgment

Special thanks to Ashvin Raj, Deepthi L and the whole Booksthakam family for standing by my side, offering incredible support, and helping me bring this book to life.

I would also like to express my heartfelt gratitude to my dear friend, Anjali, for being the first reader of these stories, offering valuable suggestions, and dedicating your time to my work.

To everyone who supported and encouraged me to start and continue my writing, I am forever grateful. There are some people I cannot forget—without their support, my writing journey would not have been possible.

One Hour

Ebin sat in his room, phone pressed to his ear, the quiet hum of the conversation hanging in the air. The room around him felt like a reflection of his mind—cluttered and chaotic. Notices and plans covered the walls, sketches of past projects mixed with half-done ideas. At the same time, stickers and posters haphazardly lined the corners. Despite the bright daylight streaming outside, the room felt heavy and dim, the doors and windows shut tight, as though keeping the world at bay.

Ebin moved slowly, almost mechanically, as he prepared to leave. His eyes briefly flicked to his scattered belongings, but he didn't seem to fully notice them. His focus was elsewhere, lost in the conversation at hand.

On the other end of the line, a male voice broke the silence, sharp and matter-of-fact. "This won't work, Ebi," Avinash said, his tone steady but filled with an edge. "We need more interactions, more visibility. Your social media management is lacking, and if we want to stay afloat in this business, we need to do better—better engagement, better reach. It's the only way we'll survive."

Ebin's face fell, the weight of Avinash's words sinking in. He had known, deep down, that this moment would come—that his friend would eventually walk away—but hearing it spoken aloud still hit him hard, like a punch to the stomach. It was the confirmation of what he'd been dreading.

Ebin, quiet by nature and always more of an observer than a participant, struggled to find his voice in such moments. Even when things went wrong, when the cracks were wide enough to see, he rarely spoke up. He simply withdrew further, letting the world move around him without ever stepping in to stop it.

"I want to do more, man," Avinash continued, his voice tight with frustration. "I want to be part of a successful team, but I'm sorry... I just don't see a future here in our company. So..."

The word hung in the air, unfinished but understood.

There was a long silence before Avinash spoke again. "Hello? Are you still there?"

Ebin's voice was barely a whisper, almost lost in the static. "Okay. Take care. See you."

Avinash's frustration broke through again, sharp and biting. "This is the problem, Ebi—you never talk about anything. How do you expect to attract business, to build anything, if you don't engage?"

Ebin remained silent, the words lodged somewhere deep inside him, impossible to say.

After a tense moment, Avinash let out a heavy sigh. "Fine..." he muttered before ending the call.

Ebin walked over to the mirror, the reflection staring back at him with a mix of disbelief and resignation. The event management company had been his idea, his brainchild, something he had dreamed up and pitched to his friends. It had started with excitement and hope, but now it felt like an anchor pulling him down.

Avinash was the last to leave—he had stuck around the longest, and despite being aware of the issues, had made his exit. But it wasn't just about social media, Ebin knew that. The real problem had always been the mismanagement of projects by the others on the team. Avinash and his crew were responsible for the on-ground work, but their performance had been lacklustre, and it was becoming impossible to ignore.

Ebin sighed, pushing away from the mirror. He left his room, stepping over the doormat that read, 'Don't Disturb,' as if it were some subtle reminder to leave things untouched.

He washed his hands slowly, the cool water doing little to calm the storm inside him. He moved to the kitchen, his mind still running through the conversation, replaying every word. He sat down at the table, the simple act of eating breakfast now feeling more like a mechanical task than something to enjoy.

His mother, who had been watching him with quiet concern, spoke up from across the table. "Avinash called. He told me you didn't say anything when he said he was leaving. Why didn't you try to persuade him to stay?"

Ebin paused mid-bite, his gaze dropping to his plate. He wasn't sure how to respond. The words felt heavy in his mouth. Finally, he replied, his voice low, "There's nothing more to discuss."

His mother's eyes narrowed, a mix of worry and frustration in them. "Why don't you talk to him? Try to change his mind. You can't just let things fall apart without at least trying."

Ebin chewed slowly, thinking about what to say next, but his thoughts were scattered. He finished his meal in silence, then stood up, grabbing his bike keys.

His mother's voice broke through the quiet. "Why don't you ever talk to anyone? You need to reach out and seek help.

How many times have I told you this?" She sighed heavily. "Where are you going?"

Ebin paused, looking at her but offering no explanation. "I just need some peace from this chaos," he said, his tone distant, as though he were speaking more to himself than to her. Without another word, he grabbed his bike and headed for the door.

His mother watched him leave, her face full of concern, but she didn't stop him. She only sighed again, her heart heavy with the uncertainty of where he was headed—both physically and emotionally.

As Ebin rode through the city, the rush of the traffic and the noise of the streets seemed to fade away as he found himself entering a quieter part of town. He turned onto a side road and came across a bus stand tucked away, surrounded by patches of greenery. The peacefulness of the area stood in stark contrast to the chaos in his mind. Only a few people were there, all seemingly lost in their own thoughts, adding to the calm atmosphere.

Ebin parked his bike and, without a second thought, walked over to a bench and sank into it, his body feeling heavy, weighed down by the endless stream of doubts that filled his head. The air around him was quiet, yet his mind was anything but. He pulled out his phone, scrolling through his social media with a sense of detachment, as though it were just a habit rather than something he actively cared about. He stared at his feed, wondering if he was really to blame for everything falling apart. *Was Avinash right? Was my lack of engagement the cause of it all? Should I just give up on my venture altogether?*

Lost in these thoughts, he barely noticed the soft voice that broke through his reverie.

"Excuse me," the voice said, gentle but persistent.

Ebin didn't respond at first, too caught up in his swirling emotions.

"Excuse me," the voice repeated, a little louder this time, pulling him back to the present.

He lifted his head slowly, eyes still clouded with uncertainty, and met the gaze of a young woman standing before him. She was dressed in a simple white top and jeans and her presence radiated a quiet beauty and calm. Her serene demeanour stood in sharp contrast to his inner turmoil, and for a moment, Ebin couldn't help but feel drawn to her calmness.

"Is this seat taken?" she asked, her voice breaking the silence that had enveloped Ebin.

Ebin looked up, momentarily startled, and shook his head. "No, go ahead," he said quietly, his voice barely audible.

She smiled and sat down beside him, the calmness of her presence a stark contrast to the storm of thoughts swirling in Ebin's mind. He turned his gaze back to the ground, the weight of the morning's events pressing down on him. His thoughts lingered on the phone call with Avinash, the unravelling of his business, and the failure that seemed to be closing in on him.

Is this happening because I struggle to talk to people? he wondered. *Maybe mom is right. I should try to communicate more. But how can I speak when I don't want to?*

"If you don't speak, how will anyone know how you feel?" Her voice cut through his thoughts, pulling him out of his reverie.

Her words surprised him. They were exactly what he had been pondering, as if she had read his mind. He turned to look at her, his brow furrowing in confusion. But she wasn't looking at him. She was speaking into her phone, the conversation seemingly directed at someone else.

"If you have an issue with him, I can talk to him and make changes if needed," she continued, her tone calm and assured. She paused for a moment, listening, before ending the call with a soft click.

Ebin blinked, the unexpected alignment of her words and his thoughts still leaving him unsettled. He stared at her, intrigued, trying to make sense of the uncanny timing.

She looked back at him, her eyes meeting his for the first time, a small, knowing smile on her lips. "I'm a short film director," she said casually, as if the revelation wasn't a big deal. "One of my cast members had a problem with a co-star, so I'm responsible for sorting it out."

Ebin, still processing the strange synchronicity of their interaction, returned her smile with a small, tentative one of his own.

"What do you do?" she asked, her voice light, her curiosity genuine.

"Until this morning, I was an entrepreneur. Now, I guess I'm unemployed," Ebin admitted, his voice low, tinged with uncertainty.

"Oh, I'm sorry to hear that. What happened?" she asked, her tone warm and understanding, though there was curiosity in her eyes.

Ebin hesitated, his thoughts scattered. "I'm not entirely sure. We weren't getting good projects or interactions. My friends backed out, and... it's over now, I suppose." His words trailed off, as if the weight of his failure was too much to carry in a single breath.

He realized, suddenly, that he had opened up to a complete stranger. The feeling caught him off guard, leaving him a bit vulnerable. He fell silent, unsure of what to say next, his mind returning to the doubts his mother had planted in him. *Was she right?* The question hovered in the back of his mind, unanswered.

"What was your entrepreneurship, by the way?" she asked, a shift in her tone signalling genuine interest.

Ebin rubbed the back of his neck, feeling the tension creep back into his shoulders. "It's all over anyway, so it doesn't matter now." He tried to avoid delving deeper, hoping to change the subject.

But the air between them hung thick with unspoken thoughts, and Ebin, feeling the discomfort of the conversation, considered leaving. He glanced around, feeling the desire to escape from the weight of the moment.

Understanding his unease she seemed to soften, her tone shifting to something more personal. "My short film is on the verge of falling through," she said, a trace of frustration in her voice. "My producer backed out at the last minute."

Ebin looked at her, his curiosity piqued by the shift in the conversation. "Finding a new producer must be tough," he said, his voice more engaged now.

"It is," she replied, her gaze steady as she met his. "But I work with new people often. It gives me a chance to gain broader exposure for my projects and learn from different perspectives. Sometimes, that's exactly what I need to keep going."

"How do you find new people consistently?" Ebin asked, genuinely curious.

She smiled, a hint of pride in her answer. "I use social media," she explained, her tone casual. "An attractive page with good content opens doors for conversations."

Ebin absorbed her words, thinking it over for a moment. Then, she added, "Don't be so tense. I wasn't always this confident. Two years ago, I was shy and uncertain. I lacked the courage to pursue my passions. But a breakup... it helped me find my strength." She smiled softly, a hint of nostalgia in her eyes. "I say I'm two years old now, because that's how much I've grown since then. My first short film even won me 'Best Director'."

She reached into her bag and pulled out her phone, quickly showing him her website. "I really love how it's designed," she said, her voice filled with pride.

Ebin glanced at the screen, his interest piqued. "I do freelance website design for various clients," he remarked.

Her eyes widened with excitement. "Really?" she asked, pausing for a beat. Then, a playful tone crept into her voice. "Wait... Don't say you designed this website?"

"But I'm afraid, yes, it was me," Ebin replied, smiling.

She laughed softly. "Wow, what are the odds of that?"

The laughter lingered for a moment, and then her expression softened, her voice growing more thoughtful. "You're really good at what you do. I think your friends misjudged you," she said gently.

Ebin's smile faded, and a quiet pause filled the air, the weight of her words sinking in.

She continued, her voice softer now, "Sometimes, it's not about us. It's about the people around us, the environment we're in.

We think we have to change to fit in, but that's not how it works. You're already beautiful, creative, and enough just as you are." She looked at him, her gaze unwavering. "It's not you who needs to change—it's the world that should adapt to you. The world should be more welcoming to everyone, just as they are.

He simply smiled, a quiet relief washing over him. It was something he had longed to hear, yet no one had ever said it to him before. A person who had always spoken only to himself, in front of the mirror, was now speaking openly to a stranger.

As they continued talking, the conversation flowed more easily than Ebin had expected. There was something about her presence—something calming—that made it easier for him to open up. Before he knew it, he found himself sharing his projects, his hopes, and his entrepreneurial dreams with her—something he had never done so freely.

Time seemed to slip by unnoticed. After a while, she glanced at her watch and said, "It's been an hour. I should get going now." They both stood up, the quiet end of their unexpected connection settling in.

"Thanks for the conversation," Ebin said, his voice soft but sincere.

"It was nice talking to you. By the way, what's your name?" she asked, a curious smile tugging at her lips.

"Ebin," he replied, his own smile genuine and warm.

"I'm Sansa. How old are you?" she asked, her tone playful, as if inviting him to share something more than just facts.

"One hour," Ebin answered, his smile widening.

Sansa laughed, and at that moment, something inside Ebin clicked. For the first time in a long while, he felt a deep sense of peace and hope. It was as if the weight he'd been carrying had been gently lifted. With the new insights and the kindness he had received, a quiet confidence began to grow within him. He knew he could move forward with renewed clarity and purpose.

Raymond

In a parallel world, a boy, somewhere between 8 and 10 years old, lies half-naked in the middle of a desolate desert. His skin is battered with wounds, and his body seems exhausted. The air is still, with only an occasional mild breeze whispering by. There's nothing in sight—no plants, no animals, no signs of life. Just the boy, alone.

After some time, a middle-aged man appears, dressed in flowing robes, with a long beard and hair, his face serene. His presence seems to light up the empty landscape, an aura of calmness radiating from him. He walks toward the boy, carrying a pashmina.

Saint: "Get up, my child. Take this robe and cover yourself."

The boy slowly rises, wincing in pain, and with some difficulty, takes the robe. He dresses and sits down, staring around, confused. The saint offers him a small cup of water, which the boy drinks gratefully.

Boy: "Where is this place?"

Saint: "This is our planet. Delta."

Boy (impatiently, glancing at the saint with growing suspicion): "I know that. But... where is everyone? Where is my family? My mom, my dad, my sister... where are they?"

He looks up at the saint, his eyes narrowing, a new thought crossing his mind.

Boy (accusatory): "Did you... kidnap me?"

The saint chuckles softly, his eyes kind but knowing.

Saint: "No, my dear. I will explain. But first, tell me... what's your name?"

Ray hesitates for a moment, still unsure, then finally speaks, his voice faint.

Boy: "I'm Ray."

Saint: "Ray, what a wonderful name." (He smiles gently.) "Shall we take a walk?"

Ray nods weakly, and they begin walking together. The air is still, and the silence between them feels heavy. After a while, the saint speaks again, his voice steady and calm.

Saint: "Let me tell you something, Ray."

Ray looks up at him, sensing the shift in tone.

Saint: "Millions of years ago, our planet was a lifeless desert. Nothing but dust and stone. Over time, small plants began to sprout. After many years, tiny creatures emerged. They lived, evolved, grew, and filled this planet. And for a long time, Delta was the only planet with life."

Boy: "They lived? If they lived here, where are they now?"

The saint pauses, giving Ray a soft, knowing smile.

Saint: "Let me explain."

Ray winces in pain, struggling to walk.

Boy: "Can we sit down? I think I've hurt my leg..."

The saint gestures to a nearby rock, and they sit. He carefully helps Ray, massaging his leg, cleaning it gently.

Saint: "Do you know about the dynamos?"

Boy: "Yes! I've studied them. I've seen their skeletons in the museum. They were huge! Some could fly, others could swim. They could have killed us if they were still alive."

Saint (nodding): "Yes, the mighty dynamos. They ruled the planet once, their power unmatched. But like many creatures, they grew too proud, driven by hunger and need. And—"

Boy (interrupting, a bit puzzled): "But... what about the other animals? Couldn't they have helped? Like how you helped me get up?"

Saint (smiling gently, then pausing momentarily): "It's not always so simple. The dynamos, like many before them, were in conflict with the world around them. They were too focused on their own survival, and the balance of nature couldn't be restored."

The boy nods slowly.

The saint gently checks Ray's leg, his hands moving carefully over the injury, assessing it with a soft, concerned expression.

Saint: "Just get up. See how it feels now?"

Ray hesitates but tries to stand, testing his leg carefully.

Ray: "Yeah, I'm okay now, I think. Let's walk..."

The saint puts his hand over Ray's shoulder, and they begin walking again.

Saint: "Now, let me tell you what happened to them."

Saint: "They fought. And in the end, it was nature itself that decided enough was enough. Disasters—great storms, volcanic eruptions, plagues—sped up their extinction. Nature did not spare them. They could no longer survive, and they vanished."

Boy (after a pause, looking up at the saint with disbelief): "That's how the mighty dynamos died?"

Saint: "Yes, the mighty dynamos. They disappeared. Like I said, many creatures like them have come and gone. Some lived for thousands of years, others only a short time. Some had wings, some swam, and others walked. But all of them eventually faded away."

Ray is quiet for a moment, staring into the distance.

Saint (with a gentle laugh): "You see, child, the world is not always so simple."

As they continue walking, Ray's attention starts to drift. He absentmindedly runs his fingers over the pashmina the saint has given him, his thoughts wandering.

Boy (softly, almost to himself): "This shawl reminds me of my mom's. I always used to play with it when she sat by me."

He pauses, staring at the shawl, his expression turning distant as memories flood back. After a moment, he looks up, his voice tinged with sadness.

Boy: "Oh, I miss her so much. And now... I'm in the middle of a history class with nowhere to go."

His gaze shifts to the saint, his eyes filled with a quiet desperation.

Boy: "Hey, can you help me find my mother?"

The saint nods, his eyes reflecting understanding, and he smiles softly, sensing the pain behind Ray's words.

Saint: "I thought you might be interested in knowing about our planet, the dynamos, and all the other creatures."

Ray's frustration becomes evident as he fidgets with the shawl, his voice sharp.

Ray (irritated): "Yes, it was interesting at first. But not now."

The saint's smile remains, patient and calm.

Saint: "Then let me tell you about another creature, one you might be familiar with. I'm sure you'll find it more interesting."

Ray (curious, but still distracted): "What is it?"

Saint: "Humans. The mighty humans."

Ray lets out a short laugh, shaking his head.

Ray: "Mighty? We're not mighty. The dynamos were mighty. Have you seen their skeletons? Or the blue aqua titan, the giant fish? Now those were mighty."

The saint smiles gently, as though he's heard this response many times before.

Saint: "But many humans thought they were the mightiest creatures on Delta. And in their own way, they were."

He begins walking slowly, as if weighing his next words carefully.

Ray: "Hey, slow down. What happened to us?"

The saint pauses, turning back to Ray, his face calm but thoughtful.

Saint: "Humans were just another species, who arrived millions of years after the plants and creatures. But they had something no other creature had—a powerful mind. A mind that allowed them to build cities, conquer the land, and shape the world around them. But in their pride, they thought they could control everything."

Ray nods slowly, absorbing what the saint has said. His expression is more contemplative now, as the pieces of the world around him begin to fall into place.

Saint: "Do you know what all living things need to survive?"

Boy: "Air, water, food... toys... maybe? I'm not sure."

The saint laughs softly, his voice warm.

Saint: "Yes, that's right, my child. But where do they get these things?"

Boy: "Mostly from plants, right? And animals too."

Saint: "Very good. You're quite a smart boy."

He continues, his tone shifting to something more serious.

Saint: "The plants give them air, food, shelter—everything they need. But instead of respecting that balance, humans began to take more and more. They cut down forests, hunted animals, and changed the world to suit their needs."

Boy: "But if they depend on the plants, why would they destroy them? It would affect us, right?"

Ray shifts uncomfortably, his mind clearly troubled by what he's hearing. The saint, noticing this, gestures to a nearby rock. They sit down together.

Saint: "As humans grew in number, it became harder for them to rule themselves. So, they divided into groups. They created classifications based on race, job, or beliefs. And those divisions led to hatred. To violence. One group thought it was superior to another—and that's when the fighting began."

Boy: "So, they fought each other?"

The saint nods slowly, his expression solemn.

Saint: "Yes. For generations. They waged wars, took land, hurt one another—all to protect their own power. And in the process, they were destroying the plants, the animals, and the very planet they depended on. The hatred grew stronger. They fought for control, following their own rules, abusing one another."

Ray's face shows confusion and disbelief.

Ray: "Which group was more dangerous?"

The saint looks at him, his eyes filled with sadness.

Saint: "Everyone. Except the ones who loved each other. The rest... they were all destroying the plants, disturbing the animals' habitats. Slowly, creatures began to vanish."

Boy (disappointed): "How could they do that? How could they just destroy everything? How cruel! What did those creatures do to deserve to go extinct? And how could they just destroy things for their needs? You said they arrived just recently, and the plants and other things were here first!"

The saint lowers his head slightly, sadness in his expression as he takes in Ray's words. He looks down for a moment, reflecting, before speaking slowly.

Saint: "They were not just destroying the plants. They were at war with one another... for power, for control, for their own interests... their own groups."

Ray's confusion deepens, his brow furrowing as he processes this information.

Ray: "Protect their group? But you said these groups and classes were made millions of years ago just to govern people. And you're saying they're still following that?"

The saint smiles, a soft, knowing smile, but his eyes carry a weight of sorrow.

Saint: "Yes."

Ray looks incredulously at the saint, shaking his head in disbelief.

Ray (angry): "No... you're lying!"

The saint remains calm, not defensive, but simply observant.

Ray (frustrated): "You told me they were mighty! You said they had legs, brains full of determination... and now you're telling me they're still following something that existed millions of years ago? It's not even something that existed back then—they created it for themselves!"

The saint lets out a small chuckle, soft and gentle.

Saint: "You're a smart kid."

Ray stares at him, clearly still confused.

Ray: "No... everyone understands this."

Ray stands up quickly, his agitation increasing.

Saint: "Actually, no."

The boy pauses, as if the saint's words might be pointing toward something much worse. Ray hesitates, his expression a mixture of confusion and reluctance, like he's not sure whether he's ready to hear more.

Ray: "You're just making up stories. I'm going to find my family on my own."

The saint watches him carefully, then speaks softly, his tone still kind but firm.

Saint: "Wait... let me finish. Come, sit with me."

Ray hesitates for a moment but slowly sits back down. The saint waits, giving him the time he needs to settle, then continues in the same calm voice.

Saint: "Sometimes, child, the desire for power blinds even the wisest beings. The more they fought, the more they destroyed. It wasn't just the plants or animals they hurt—it was the balance of the entire world."

Ray (frustrated): "But you said humans were powerful! They had brains, they could think! Why didn't they stop?"

The saint smiles, but there's sadness in his eyes, a deep understanding of the complexity of the situation.

Saint: "Some did try, Ray. Some tried to warn others, tried to make them see the danger. But power is a dangerous thing, and those who held it did not listen. They suppressed the warnings, dismissed them. And in the end..."

The saint's voice trails off, as if the weight of the truth is too much to continue. Ray looks at him, his mind struggling to understand. The air feels heavier as he absorbs the silence, waiting for the saint to speak again.

Ray, shocked by the weight of the words, slowly sits back down, his face pale as the realization sets in.

Ray: "In the end... they... destroyed themselves?"

The saint nods solemnly, the gravity of his words sinking in.

Saint: "Yes, Ray. A great disaster came, and the human race vanished."

Ray's world seems to collapse around him. The pieces of the story he had feared were true—his mind had been unwilling to fully accept them. His eyes well up with tears, his heart heavy with the loss of everything he knows.

Ray: "No... my parents... they didn't do anything wrong! Why are they gone? Please, bring them back!"

The saint moves closer, pulling Ray into an embrace. He strokes his back gently, offering a moment of solace as the boy cries, the raw grief pouring out. The saint remains silent, allowing Ray to process, offering him water and a chance to release the pain.

Saint (softly): "I know, child. I know. But sometimes... crying won't change what has happened. Life moves on, even after great loss."

After a while, Ray slowly begins to calm down. He wipes his eyes, still struggling to believe the truth, but now more willing to accept it. He looks up at the saint, his voice quiet but full of confusion.

Ray: "But... why didn't they see the danger? Why didn't they change?"

The saint takes a deep breath, his voice gentle yet filled with sorrow as he speaks again.

Saint: "They were too caught up in their own power. And by the time they saw the truth, it was too late. But... there is still hope."

Ray looks up at him, his expression confused and uncertain, trying to understand.

Ray: "What do you mean? The humans are gone... everything is gone."

The saint smiles softly, a glimmer of reassurance in his eyes. He points to the ground beneath them. Ray looks down, puzzled, wondering what the saint means.

A small, green sprout begins to push through the barren soil. A small lake, shimmering in the distance, appears to materialize almost as if out of nowhere. The soft ripples from the water touch Ray's legs, pulling him out of his thoughts.

The saint looks at the sprouting plant, then at the lake, his expression soft with understanding.

Saint: "Even after the greatest destruction, life finds a way to begin again. Nature always leaves behind a seed of hope."

Ray stares at the sprout for a long moment. The water laps gently against his legs. It's almost like he's seeing it for the first time, as though the landscape has shifted while he wasn't paying attention. He blinks slowly, his mind clearing, as if he's just coming out of a fog.

The sensation of the cool water pulls him back into the present. The quiet stillness lingers for a moment longer as the surroundings feel almost unreal. He looks down at the water, and the word slips from his lips.

Ray (quietly): "Raymond. My name is Raymond."

There's a pause. The saint, watching him with a calm gaze, offers a soft smile, as though recognizing the shift in Ray's awareness.

Saint: "Yes, Raymond. A ray of hope."

The Best

(Author's caution: Shankar's got a lot on his mind—literally. Pay attention, or you might start hearing things too!)

Shankar:

Hey, this is Shankar, I'm 28 years old and a banker at the New India Development Finance Corporation (NDFC)......

(he was interrupted by the other voice)

Shankar Bother:

Wait a second, Shanku! Is this the way you're going to introduce yourself to a new friend? Come on, give them more details! Don't be so vague.

Shankar Brother:

What's wrong with this? This is enough for an introduction! Why should one throw everything out there on the first try? Let them get to know you slowly.

Shankar:

Okay, okay. You might be wondering who these 'Shankar Bother' and 'Shankar Brother' are.

Well, they're actually my inner voices. They're like two distinct personalities, always talking to me. "Bother" is the more supportive one, always helping me with my ideas and motivations, and, let me be honest, he likes to call me 'Shanku' all the time. I don't mind it though — I kind of like it too.

But then there's 'Brother'. He's a bit different — more soft spoken and a little too simple for my liking. He calls me 'Shankar'.

Shankar Bother:

Enough with the explanation, fool! Introduce yourself properly to your readers.

Shankar:

Alright! Fine. Here it goes:

Hey, I'm Shankar Swaminathan, 27 and a half years young. I work as a Branch Manager at NDFC, Colaba Branch, Mumbai. I'm not married, and yes, I'm single. So, to any girls reading this — if you're single, you can hit me up on Instagram @thebestshankarswami.

Shankar Brother:

Sigh... Really, Shankar?

Shankar Bother:

Haha, that's a good one, Shanku! By the way, it was good that you mentioned you are single. Kavya, your girlfriend, she's just a receptionist, man. She's really not 'your type' for your current status. Look at Arun's girlfriend — she's an IT professional and skilled in hacking. You need to step up your game, Shanku. Maybe start by updating your relationship status. Time to move on, buddy!

Shankar:

What do you think, Brother?

Shankar Brother:

Kavya loves you, Shankar. That's all that matters. Don't compare her to anyone, especially not with Arun. Why even bring him into this? You've been in a race with him since school, but he probably doesn't even realize it.

Shankar Bother:

Shut up, Brother! You don't know anything! You don't get it! Arun is the real problem. He's the one causing all the trouble for Shanku. Readers need to know about this idiot, Arun Prakash. Come on, Shanku, tell them about him!

Shankar:

Alright, alright.

Arun was my schoolmate and childhood friend. He came to my school after 8th grade. I'll admit it — he's good looking, and everyone likes him, including the teachers. My best friend also likes him more than me. He's good at sports, academics, you name it. It felt like he was better than me at everything, and I hated it. I wanted to outshine him, but he was just so damn perfect.

That's when Bother said to me:

'The best way to beat your rival is by making them your friend.'

So, I became friends with Arun. I tried to understand him, figure him out. He's got this vulnerable side, you know? He's empathetic and helps people when they're in need.

But even with all that, I couldn't beat him in academics — especially in the 9th and 10th grades. I had to admit defeat. When the time came for us to choose our streams in Plus One, I saw that Arun was going for Science. I didn't want to compete anymore, so I took Commerce. Big relief.

Arun was also good at drama, acting, and mimicry. He had a special talent for it, no doubt. And, oh yeah, he's an incredible football player. I didn't even know that until I saw him play for the school team and win 'Player of the Match'. It turns out he was on the district team! But he never mentioned that before. How weird is that?

Shankar Brother:

Weird? You call that weird? Remember that time you won the first prize in the frog jump competition at the residence association, and the very next day, you gave your school friends a treat? That's weird, not what Arun did.

Shankar: *(pretending to avoid what Brother just said)*

Anyway, Arun had a ton of female fans, so I thought, 'Why not become more friendly with girls too?' That's what I did. I became somewhat popular for a while, and I was proud of it... until I realized why they were really fond of me. They'd come to me saying,

'Hey, Shanku, can you introduce us to Arun?'

'Hey, Shanku, can you give us Arun's number?'

Shankar Bother:

Crap!

Shankar:

True story, now let me tell you about one school election that really stood out, during our 12th grade..., I was nervous that Arun would nominate himself. But guess what? He didn't. Why? He was probably scared of competing with me, right?

Shankar Brother was about to say something but decided not to speak.

Shankar Bother:

Oh, listen, Saint Brother intends to share his wisdom. Please, share, my lord. *(Shankar Bother mocked him.)*

Shankar Brother:

It's not that he was afraid of you, Shankar. At that time, even his friends and the principal told him to put his name in for the nomination, but he refused because you told him first that you wanted to nominate yourself. It's not because of fear, it's because of what you said earlier, remember? He's vulnerable and empathetic in relationships. That's the reason.

Shankar Bother:

Doofus! I've told you a million times—don't talk to Shanku like that! Who do you think you are?!

Shankar Bother was clearly irritated, his face reddening with frustration. He couldn't take it anymore and snapped back sharply.

Shankar:

Hey, hey, hey, please stop, guys. Let me finish the story, please.

Shankar Bother:

Only because Shanku asked me to, I'm stopping. Alright, go on, dear.

Shankar:

So, things didn't exactly stop there. I worked hard and scored 92% in Plus Two, while Arun, as always, edged ahead with 95%. But hey, I had my own share of victories. I ended up with Sreya, while Arun had Anjali. For a while, I thought things were falling into place. Then, I met Maneesha... and Arun? Well, he still had Anjali. But eventually, things changed for him. I got Kavya... and, well, guess what? I won. Arun and Anjali broke up. I thought, 'Finally, I've beaten him at something.'

But even when I thought I had one up on him, it always felt like he had an answer for everything.

When college came around, it was a little different. We went to separate colleges, but I still called him often, just like I always did.

Shankar Bother:

That's my boy! Tell them about your next win!

Shankar:

Right after college, I got campus selection at NDFC as a trainee.

Shankar Bother:

And Arun? What was he doing at that time?

Shankar:

He was preparing for the Police SI exam.

And two years later, I got promoted to Clerk at NDFC.

Shankar Bother:

What was Arun doing then?

Shankar:

Still preparing for the exam.

Shankar Bother (*laughs*):

What was he doing when you got promoted to Assistant Branch Manager?

Shankar:

Same thing. He was still preparing for the exam.

(They both laugh.)

Shankar Brother:

Hey, Shankar. Want to share what happened after you got promoted to Assistant Branch Manager?

Shankar Bother:

Oh no, don't listen to him. Just focus on your own thing.

Shankar: (*sighs*)

Okay, here's the twist... Arun topped the state in the Police SI exam that year.

Shankar Brother:

How did you find out?

Shankar: (*pauses, his voice heavy*)

A flex board went up right in front of my branch... congratulating him: 'Congratulations Arun Prakash for securing first rank in the SI exam, from Win Academy students and teachers.'

Shankar Brother:

Alright, Shankar. It's great that you finally decided to share this. Now, go ahead, continue your story.

Shankar:

But I didn't give up, guys. That's the main thing about me. After he got his job, I called him for a treat. After so many calls, plans, and last-minute cancellations, he finally agreed to treat me—months after he got his job. As we were on our way to the restaurant, Arun said, '*Anjali told me to say hi to you.*'

I forced a smile and said, '*Oh, yes! I heard you guys patched things up.*' I quickly changed the topic, trying to sound casual: '*By the way, have you started filing your ITR?*'

Arun: '*No, Shankar, I haven't yet. My LPA isn't above the permissible limit, but yeah, I should probably file it anyway.*'

Shankar:

I thought to myself at that moment, 'Yes, I beat him again. His salary is below 5LPA, and mine's almost double—10LPA.' After dinner, just to rub it in, I paid the bill and said, '*No worries, Arun. I've got it covered. I didn't realize SI officers were paid so little.*'

Shankar Bother:

Again you won!

Shankar:

Yeah, I did. Thanks for your help too.

Bother grinned with a devilish look, clearly enjoying the moment.

Shankar:

But I was really surprised when I heard the news the next day after the treat. It said: '*Accolades to SI Arun Prakash and his team. The SI and his team had gone undercover to infiltrate a counterfeit currency syndicate circulating fake notes within the local economy. Posing as a buyer, the SI gained access to the counterfeit printing operation and worked with the police to gather evidence of the syndicate's operations, including links to international crime organizations.*' *It also added,* '*To avoid public panic over the circulation of fake currency, authorities delayed the media report until all operations were shut down and the full scope of the syndicate's activities was understood. The operation had taken place a month ago.*'

Shankar takes a sip of water, looking back at that moment.

Shankar:

I remember thinking, even though we had dinner just the night before, he hadn't mentioned a thing about this. This had happened a month ago, right? What is it with that guy? After all these years, I still couldn't outshine him. No matter what, he always comes back stronger. And somehow, I always fall short. Weird, right?

Shankar Bother:

Oh, don't use the word 'weird' when talking about Saint Arun. His guru, this 'Brother' guy, won't like that.

(he mocks Shankar Brother again)

Shankar Brother:

Your story's over, right? Enough of this nonsense, Shankar. Why bother yourself so much? These things happened years back now leave these things, you do your thing, let him do his. You guys are 28 now, not kids anymore.

Shankar ignores the conversation as his phone rings.

Shankar:

Wait, wait, Sooraj is calling me back.

Shankar answers the call and talks to Sooraj.

Shankar Brother:

Do you know why he called Sooraj?

Shankar Bother:

Yeah, to tell Sooraj that he got promoted to Branch Manager.

Shankar Brother:

Did Sooraj ask about it?

Shankar Bother:

Obviously not.

Shankar Brother:

This guy won't change. Did he tell Arun about this?

Shankar Bother:

I told him to call. I think he did, but Arun didn't pick up.

Shankar comes back with a smile: "Guys, guess what?"

Shankar Bother:

What?

Shankar:

Arun has resigned from his job. *(Laughs loudly)*

Shankar Bother:

We won! We won! At last! You're a six-figure earning Branch Manager, and he's unemployed! (*Shankar Bother yells excitedly*)

Shankar:

Five years ago, when he got the job, my sleep was over. Everyone kept talking about him, praising his valour, and the news just wouldn't stop. But now, he's resigned. Big relief. Finally, I should celebrate!

Meanwhile, Shankar Brother is checking Instagram, smiling to himself.

Shankar:

(*looking confused)*

What's in that, brother? What's there to smile about?

Shankar Brother:

(smiling)

I was just checking Arun's Insta stories, Shankar. Two updates caught my eye. First, he's marrying Anjali, you know, the IT professional and hacker, and FYI, she is the one who helped him solve that case too. And second, he's going to direct a film with Mr. Surya, the actor, in the lead role!

Shankar:

What??

Shankar Bother:

What??

Shankar freezes.

The words hit him like a punch to the gut. His eyes widen in disbelief. For a moment, everything stands still as the reality of the situation sinks in.

Shankar:

(softly, to himself)

So, that's why Arun resigned from his job...

Shankar Bother:

(leaning in, surprised)

Really? Arun? That guy? What does he even know about all this?

Shankar Brother:

(taunting)

Your 'Shanku' told us earlier, right? From their school days, Arun always had this 'special talent for drama and acting'. So, why can't this happen?

Shankar Bother:

(cursing)

Darn it.

Shankar:

(agitated)

Darn it! What do I do now?

Shankar Brother:

(nonchalantly)

What's there to do? Just call him and say congratulations. That's it.

Shankar Bother:

(angrily)

Hello, professor! Don't be such a nice guy, okay? Shankar should congratulate Arun? Really? Are you out of your mind? I'm scared to see where this is going.

Shankar:

(confused)

Where?

Shankar Bother:

(dramatically)

Directing a film... making it a hit... everyone acknowledging him. Now he's going to direct a film with Surya, later Vijay, Rajinikanth, Shahrukh Khan, and then DiCaprio one day?

Shankar:

(*shocked*)

DiCaprio??

Shankar Bother:(*he continues his exaggeration*)

Everyone acknowledges him—State Awards, National Awards... or maybe... Oscars? Oh God, I can't face this!

Shankar:

(eyes widening, increasingly tense)

Oscars??

(*Shankar starts pacing, visibly distressed*)

Oh no! What do I do now, Bother?

(*The tension builds as Shankar becomes more panicked.)*

Bother?

Bother?

(There's a long pause with no reply.)

Shankar Brother:

(smiles)

It seems your companion fainted, Shankar.

Shankar:

(desperate)

Hey, Brother, please help me!

Shankar Brother:

(teasing)

Oh, so you need my help now?

Shankar:

Please don't kick me now!

Shankar Brother:

(sighing)

Okay, tell me this — what did Arun do wrong to you?

Shankar:

(resentful)

First, he took my best friend, who was with me all through school until 8th standard. Everyone liked Arun, even the teachers!

Shankar Brother:

(cutting in)

Is that his problem?

Shankar:

I don't know.

Shankar Brother:

(leaning in)

Okay, tell me this — you mentioned an election during your 12th grade days. Who won the election?

Shankar:

(meekly)

Me.

Shankar Brother:

How?

Shankar:

(quietly)

Arun helped me.

Shankar Brother:

(sarcastically)

Of course, Arun helped. Now, why did Anjali and Arun break up?

Shankar:

(avoiding eye contact)

I... I planned behind their backs. Made up some story that made Anjali break up with him.

Shankar Brother:

(raises an eyebrow)

Classic move. How did you get Kavya then?

Shankar:

(sighs)

Kavya is Anjali's friend. Arun knew it, so... he set me up.

Shankar Brother:

(firmly)

Okay. Have you noticed over the last five years — how many times Arun called you?

Shankar:

(shrugs)

No.

Shankar Brother:

(raising his hand)

Zero. And do you know how many times he picked up your call on the first try?

Shankar:

(frowning)

No... he never picks it up on the first try. Always the second or third.

Shankar Brother:

You are so dumb enough that you didn't understand he doesn't like your call. That's why he didn't pick up your call on the first try.

Shankar (*sadly*):

How dare he do this to me! I'm the best... I'll show him. Brother, tell me, what should I do to beat him again?

Shankar Brother

(sighs and said)

Will you do whatever I say?

Shankar:

Yes, I will. You're incredible. I get it now. Tell me, I want to beat him!

Shankar Brother:

Pakka?

Shankar:

Yes, Brother. Believe me.

Shankar Brother:

Ok, then die! (*he said abruptly)*

Shankar:

(eyes wide open in disbelief of what he just heard)

What?!

Shankar Brother:

Yes, you should die.

Shankar:

(sad and surprised)

Hey, how can you say something like that to me? You're a peaceful guy! You're not the kind of person who usually says such evil things. Did you change characters with Bother?

Shankar Brother:

(firmly)

It's not that I switched characters with Bother. I gave you a chance just a little while ago, and I've always given you advice and chances. But you never wanted to hear me. You always listened to Bother instead.

Shankar:

(depressed and sad)

You really think I should die?

Shankar Brother:

I don't think there's an issue with Arun. It seems like you're making up all these things—calling everyone and telling them you were promoted to Bank Manager, that you went to Thailand, met new people. Yes, these things are good for you, but why make such a big deal out of them, and bother others?

Shankar:

(sighs)

You really think I should die? Can I just go into exile?

Shankar Brother:

(after thinking for a second)

I think that also works. But, because it's you, you'll probably call everyone while you're in exile and tell them how amazing it is—how you're 'in exile' and how beautiful your new girlfriend is there. Will you do that?

Shankar:

(thinking for a moment, clearly sad, without answering)

Shankar Brother:

(interrupts)

Yes, you will.

Shankar:

(quietly, admitting)

Yes... I think I will.

Shankar Brother was silent.

Shankar:

(crying)

Yes, the right thing is to die. I don't want to be in this world, seeing Arun win everything he touches. I just can't.

Shankar Brother quietly listens to everything.

Shankar:

I am going to jump off from this building. Will I die from here?

Shankar Brother:

Yes, you probably will. We are on the 7th floor, right?

Shankar:

Ok then, this is it. I will miss you guys for sure. Tell Bother too.

Shankar Brother:

(hears without saying anything in return, giving an unspoken farewell)

Shankar:

Should I post my suicide note on Instagram?

Shankar Brother:

(in disbelief and anger)

No need. Please, just... die. (puts hands together as if praying)

Shankar is about to die when, suddenly, Shankar Bother wakes from his faint.

Shankar Bother:

Shanku...!! Please don't die! (he yells)

Shankar:

(wipes his tears, happy to see Bother back)

Oh, you came back at last! Thank you—only you have love for me. At least you said not to die.

Shankar Bother:

Yes, Shanku. Please don't die like this in an ordinary way.

(Shankar gets confused)

Can we jump out of a plane? You are the best, Shanku! Die the best way!

Shankar Brother:

(laughs sarcastically, placing his hand on his forehead)

Oh, for god's sake...

(pauses, then turns away, shaking his head and walking off)

Beyond the Classroom

Even after my sessions were over, I often spent extra time with my students, talking to them, listening to their problems, and offering the solutions I could. I'm Rohit, a UPSC aspirant and mentor at the MANTRA Institute, a well-known academy for UPSC, state exams, and banking exams. The institute is located on the third floor of a building owned by the Taj Group of Companies.

One afternoon, I was sitting alone in the staffroom after my classes had ended and I'd chatted with some students. Almost all the other faculty had left, and only a few students remained. That was when Pallavi walked in—dressed in a green churidar, her expressive eyes reflecting some unspoken concern. She was a student from the state exam batch. Even though her class had started three months ago, we had never spoken before.

"Please come in, Pallavi. Have a seat," I said, noticing her standing hesitantly by the door.

Many students had trouble initiating a conversation with their mentors, so I usually talked about random things to make them feel at ease before diving into the main issue. The reason she had come to talk to me was that I was her senior at college—specifically, Mahatma Gandhi College. But I hadn't seen her. So, I assumed that some other juniors whom I had mentored before might have told her about me.

As we started talking, I learned that Pallavi was facing a dilemma that many aspirants struggle with: mental pressure. The real issue, though, was her passion for dance. She hesitated for a moment before pulling out her phone, showing me videos and pictures of her classical dance performances from college and school.

She scrolled through a few, her eyes lighting up as she spoke about the dances she had performed, the dedication it took, and the joy it brought. I could hear the excitement in her voice, but there was also a quiet longing, a hint of something unspoken—something she wasn't sure she could pursue fully.

As the pictures and videos continued, I couldn't help but feel impressed. There was a grace in her movements, a certain confidence in her posture.

"*She's good at this,*" I thought to myself, a part of me wishing she could see the potential in herself that I saw.

But she was afraid of relying on dance as a career because, for her, it didn't offer the financial stability she thought she needed. Her parents, both government servants, had always lived by the belief that a secure government job was the only way to build a stable future. They wanted her to fit into that same box, just like them. And that's why she chose the path of becoming a government servant instead of pursuing her passion for dance.

There was a brief pause. She looked down, as if lost in her thoughts, and then suddenly, without warning, she blurted out, "I have a boyfriend... sir," she said, almost as an afterthought.

Normally, I was not a fan of being called 'sir,' but that wasn't my concern right now. I was momentarily confused. *Did*

I say something wrong? I thought. *Or Is she just trying to protect herself with this 'famous' line*?

Truly, I was taken aback by her quick statement, but I let it go, forcing myself not to pull a confused face. Instead, I asked, as casually as I could, "Okay? So is he not allowing you to study?"

"No, not at all. He's very supportive. In fact, he's the one who encouraged me to join this course. But sometimes, he gets a bit overbearing," she said, irritation creeping into her voice.

I chuckled. "It's nice to have people who have your back."

She continued, "He has his own business ideas and plans. He believes I should focus on finding a proper job, not dance. He's freelancing, and he thinks I'll be doing the same if I continue to pursue my passion... so I should have a proper salaried job, to maintain our future family."

I laughed, trying to lighten the mood. The conversation went on, and I encouraged her to take her dance career seriously, but she was still fixated on getting a "secure" job. I shared my own experiences with her, promising that I would support her no matter what. After all, she was my junior and I wanted to help.

Days went by. I continued to help her with tips, solve problems, and assist her in setting a study timetable. One day, I was giving a class on "Percentages" for the banking exam batch when I overheard Mr. Deepak, the owner of the institute, yelling at the students after they had received the results of a weekly test.

"I've seen some of you hanging around in the corridors during break. What's going on? Have you studied everything? MANTRA Academy is famous for its results. No one else can compete with us. If you don't want to be in this competitive field, then leave!" he shouted.

I could sense that someone was receiving a harsh scolding from him. His voice echoed through the room. "*Yes, no matter what, we even take results from other academies to show as ours*," I thought sarcastically. Why did he have to shout at 21-year-olds about the importance of getting a job? They were adults. They knew what was at stake.

Can we talk? I'm at Broun's Café. I received a WhatsApp message from Pallavi later that evening, just as I was preparing to leave the institute.

Broun's Café was just a few meters away, and it was a place the faculty and students from the institute often went to for their coffee—it had become something of a tradition.

When I arrived, Pallavi had already ordered our coffee, but she looked upset. "Deepak sir shouted at me, sir... in front of the whole class. He insulted me. I have the lowest score in the batch."

As I listened to her, it dawned on me that the shouting I had overheard earlier was Deepak sir scolding Pallavi. I felt ashamed to face her—not because she had scored poorly, but because a mature person was being humiliated in front of the whole class, especially for just a competitive exam batch.

But honestly, the real issue was my ego. Since Pallavi was directly under my supervision, I felt responsible. It was like I had failed her too.

"Don't be sad. In the next weekly test, you're going to score well. And not just in the test—you're going to crack the main state exam next month. And get the job. This is my word!" I said, feeling a little too heroic as I grabbed my bag and stood up.

As I stepped outside, it hit me—I hadn't even touched my coffee. What a grand exit! After delivering a line like that, I couldn't very well go back and sip it now. So, I just let her finish the coffee alone. Less embarrassment that way.

Days passed, and our routine intensified. It felt like I had become her personal assistant—waking her up early, creating detailed timetables, spending hours on phone calls, and offering endless lessons. I was always there, guiding her through each step.

But as time went on, I began to wonder: *was I pushing her too hard? Was I truly helping, or was I just trying to prove something to myself*? It wasn't just about the exams anymore. Somewhere along the way, I realized that my focus might have shifted from her success to my own desire to prove I could mentor her effectively.

In between lessons, Pallavi practised her dance. Despite the pressure of our routine, those moments of joy seemed to remind me that there was more to her life than just exams.

I told myself she would never complain. After all, I was her mentor. But as the days went by, I couldn't ignore the nagging thought: *was this really for her, or was it about feeding my own ego?"*

Then, after the weekly test results came in, I found myself buried in work. Time slipped away, and I didn't check Pallavi's score until much later. Just as I was finally getting a moment to breathe, my phone buzzed with a message: "Coffee at Broun's?"

The invitation felt like a welcome distraction. I was eager to hear how she had done, and when I saw her waiting there, I couldn't hide the excitement that rushed through me.

"I'm so happy for you... Congratulations, dear!" I said, sipping my coffee. This time, I made sure I finished it before launching into any dramatic punchlines. Pallavi had become one of the toppers in the class, and I couldn't have been prouder. But I was curious to know what Deepak sir had said to her.

"That day you were upset because I shouted at you. But look at you now—my 'insult' actually made you study! So, I guess I deserve some credit for your marks," she said, mimicking Deepak sir's exact words in his voice, with a playful grin.

I laughed and replied, "Oh sure, Deepak sir can take the credit if he wants. But you and I both know who's been putting in the real work. We'll save the real celebration for when we crack the main exam next month."

She rolled her eyes, but her mood shifted. "One real happy person will be my boyfriend," she sighed.

I smiled, though I could tell she was still grappling with the pressure from him. She went on, "Yesterday, we argued again. How can someone always be positive? I'm not like that. He tells me not to worry, not to get tense, to be cool all the time. I get upset over small things, and he doesn't get it. I want to pursue dance, but he's pushing me to focus on a government job."

I didn't say anything right away. I just let her talk, casually listening while she vented.

"Why aren't you saying anything?" she asked, her voice rising a bit. "Or are you going to tell me I'm just making drama?"

"Hey, I'm your exam mentor, not your relationship coach," I replied, a little annoyed.

What's a 27-year-old single guy supposed to say to a 23-year-old, pretty girl venting about her boyfriend issues?

She probably didn't appreciate my response.

After a while, we left the café. Despite how busy the day had been, I couldn't shake the feeling that her success felt like my own. But, to my surprise, that was the last time I saw her at the academy.

The next day, as I was teaching about "Profit and Loss" to the state exam batch, I found myself scanning the room for Pallavi. She wasn't there. I tried calling her after class, but her phone was switched off. This continued for the next day as well. Finally, two days later, after my session and a small chit-chat with the students, I checked my phone and found a message from Pallavi.

"My father met with an accident two days ago while travelling to his native place. He's been in the ICU. Today they shifted him to a room."

"Oh, I'm so sorry to hear that. How is he now? Is he stable?" I replied quickly.

"Don't know. He's in a lot of pain. Two fractures in his leg and rib. I'm not sure if I'll be able to come to class this week."

"Take care of him. Don't worry about the classes. I'll handle things here when you come back," I assured her.

I understood how difficult this time would be for her; the pressure of choosing her career, the looming state exam, and now her father's serious condition. I found myself wondering if she would even be able to sit for the exam this year. Everything seemed to be stacking up against her.

The following days were quieter. Pallavi hadn't been in touch much, and I couldn't help but feel concerned. Then, after a couple of days, I got a call from her. She sounded tired, but her voice was steady as she gave me an update.

"My family and I returned home after a week," she told me. "But I'm still here with my father. He needs me, so I won't be able to come to class for a while."

I felt a pang of sympathy for her, but I knew it was her responsibility. It wasn't easy, though—being caught between caring for a loved one and trying to move forward with one's own life.

Despite everything, she still managed to study. She called me a couple of times during the week to update me on her father's condition. I admired her for pushing through, even when life seemed to be pulling her in every direction.

The exam results came out. MANTRA Academy had once again "created" great results, with many students getting selected. Chocolates and laddoos were being handed out everywhere, and it was heartwarming to see so many families celebrating their success.

It didn't surprise me that Pallavi hadn't cleared this time.

It was painful for me, but I knew I had to accept it. *Sometimes, our egos don't get what we want, and that's okay. We need to move on.* I consoled myself.

That evening, Pallavi came to see me at the café. As I waited for her, I wasn't worried about how she would take the failure. I was sure she would rise again, stronger.

She came in, congratulated me on my other students' success, and told me that some of her friends had cleared as well.

As we were sipping our favourite chocolate coffee, she said to me, "My boyfriend and I had an argument yesterday..."

I was ready to run out of the café—forget about the coffee, I couldn't tolerate another 'boyfriend story' from her, I thought.

"He thinks if I had used all my time for studying instead of practising 'silly' dance, I would have passed the exam," she said, her voice trembling. "Silly... is this how he sees my dance?" She wiped her eyes.

I took a deep breath. I listened patiently.

"I'm torn. I want to focus on dance, but I feel like I'm letting you down if I give up on the exam," she admitted, tears streaming down her face.

I touched her hand to console her. For a moment, I hesitated, unsure whether I should pull it away. Suddenly, a flood of thoughts hit me: *Am I even supposed to touch her*? Back in school, touching girls was practically a sin.

Oh,... 90s kids traumas. Get over it, idiot. You're just consoling her, not proposing marriage.

Shaking off my thoughts, I said, "Do whatever you like. It doesn't matter."

She smiled weakly. "I know you've always been there for me, supporting me. You worked hard for me, and now I feel like I'm cheating you by quitting."

I was taken aback by her words. "Oh, Pallavi... it's not about me," I said, my voice soft but firm. "Please, don't frame it like that. This isn't about my feelings. It's about you—your dreams, your happiness. I'm just here to guide you, that's all."

She looked down for a moment, gathering her thoughts before speaking again. "I know how much you cared when Deepak sir yelled at me, how you worked so hard to help me. That was for me. And now, hearing that I might let this exam go... I can't help but think it might hurt you."

"No, Pallavi. I'm actually proud of you for standing up for yourself," I said, my tone softening. "You know, I've always loved writing, but I've never really done anything about it. And look at me—here I am, mentoring and studying for UPSC. I've even forgotten what it felt like to write for myself. My English teacher used to say I was going to be an author one day, but I didn't have the courage to pursue it. But look at you. You've got that courage. That's why you're doing what you want, even if it doesn't fit into everyone's idea of success."

She looked at me, silently, so I continued.

"Not everyone fits into the box society tries to put us in, and that's okay. We don't all need to follow the same path. Securing a government job? That's not the only measure of success. What matters is peace. What matters is happiness. And yeah, sometimes being not okay is okay. It's normal to feel negative sometimes. Anyone who tells you they're happy and positive all the time? They're lying."

She stayed quiet, processing my words, and then gave me a small smile. It was the kind of smile that told me I had said exactly what she needed to hear.

.

It was getting late, and the sky had started to darken. We stayed at the café for a while, the weight of our conversation hanging in the air. Before she left, she gave me a tight hug, and in that moment, all my ego seemed to wash away. I wasn't prepared for the sudden surge of emotion.

She pulled back slightly, looked at me with a soft smile, and said, "Promise me you'll write."

I smiled back, feeling a quiet sense of peace, and replied, "I will. Good luck, Pallavi."

With that, we left the café, both of us carrying a sense of relief—like a weight had been lifted, even though the road ahead was still uncertain.

A few months later, I was in the backstage at Pallavi's dance performance when I got a call from her.

"Hey, where are you?" Pallavi asked through phone, her voice filled with excitement right after her performance

"I'm just behind the stage, talking with your brother," I replied, smiling at the thought of her performance.

Then, I saw her—dressed in her white and red Mohiniyattam attire, the fabric flowing elegantly with each step. There was something about the way she moved, so confident and graceful. Her hair was perfectly styled, a few delicate flowers tucked into her bun, complementing her serene expression. At that moment, she was every bit the dancer I had known she could be—and more.

As she spotted me, her face lit up, and she ran to me, throwing her arms around me in a tight hug. I could feel the warmth of her gratitude, and for a moment, I couldn't speak. It was as though everything had come full circle. The girl who had been unsure of her path, torn between her dreams and expectations, was now standing before me, a successful dancer with a clear sense of self.

"Thank you," she whispered, her eyes glistening with emotions.

It was the same feeling I had when I heard Pallavi had topped the class in that week's test — the same pride, the same sense of elation. I felt like I was on cloud nine.

"Congratulations! That was an amazing performance," I said, genuinely impressed.

I was at a loss for words. I smiled, feeling a wave of pride. It wasn't just because of her performance—it was the journey she'd taken to get there, the struggles she'd overcome, the balance she'd found between her passions and responsibilities.

At that moment, I realised how far we both had come. I had spent so much time guiding her, helping her through her doubts, but in a way, she had also taught me something: the importance of following your heart, no matter how difficult the path might seem.

I reached into my bag, feeling the weight of the moment. Slowly, I pulled out a small package and held it out to her. As she looked up, her curiosity evident in her eyes, I cleared my throat.

"This is a copy of my first book," I said, my voice thick with emotion. I watched her eyes widen, waiting for her reaction. "I kept it a secret, wanted to build some suspense until it was published... but now, I want you to have it."

She took it from my hands. As she unwrapped the book, her face flushed with happiness and disbelief. "You wrote this?" she asked, her voice soft with awe.

I nodded, feeling a strange mix of pride and vulnerability. "Yeah. I kept putting it off for so long, but... like you, I finally found the courage to pursue it."

Her eyes sparkled as she held the book, a sense of pride and connection between us. "I'm so proud of you, Rohit," she said, her voice steady but full of feeling.

For a brief moment, we stood there in silence, just the two of us, knowing that we had both achieved something special—something that had once seemed impossible. As she hugged me once more, I remembered and felt the weight of the years we had spent together—her struggles, my doubts, and how, in the end, we had both found our own paths. And that, I realised, was all that truly mattered.

In the Heart of an Enchanted Forest

Chapter 1

One Sunday afternoon, one of Arvind and Priya's four children, while taking a nap after playing, overhears the TV news.

The reporter says:

"Communal riots in our country have been worse than ever. In the last 24 hours, seven lives have been lost in mob attacks in various parts of our country. This is only the official count; the unofficial count is more than 15. A curfew has been announced for seven days. Schools will remain closed, and only essential shops will be open during this time. The government has denied permission for any public meetings and functions. The opposition party claims these riots are sponsored by the ruling party, as elections are approaching, and they are using religion as a weapon to divide our nation. We urge our citizens to remain united during these tough times and abide by the laws of the country."

"Yeeehh!" Nirav, one of the twins, yelled, holding a Captain America toy with him. The joy for him was that there wouldn't be school for the next week.

"Shh! Lower your voice, Nirav. Arya is sleeping," Priya scolds.

The four kids are a pair of twin boys: Nirav and Niraj, the elder ones, aged six, studying in Vikram Sarabhai Public School. Their immediate younger brother, Ishaan, is in his LKG at the same school, and Arya, their two-year-old sister, does exactly what her brothers do. Arvind and Priya are having a tough time dealing with these adorable kids, but they really enjoy it.

Every morning, a lively "battle" ensues in their household as the family gets ready for the day. Arvind takes charge of dressing himself and his boys, while Priya, multitasking with incredible skill, prepares the food and feeds them—all with little Arya nestled in her arms. By profession, Arvind is an Animation Cartoon Artist at DQ Entertainment in Hyderabad, where he brings imagination to life by working on video games, superhero movies, and children's films, blending creativity with technology to entertain and inspire.

After the boys leave for school and Arvind heads to his studio, it's officially "girls' time" in the house. Priya, with a smile, scoops Arya up and gives her a warm bath, gently placing her in a small basin filled with water. Arya's little face lights up as she splashes happily, the sound of water sloshing around filling the air. Priya watches her with affection, amused by how much Arya enjoys the simplest of things.

As Arya plays, Priya takes a deep breath and moves on to the next task—cleaning up the living room. It's a place where toys are strewn everywhere, evidence of a day full of imagination and play. There's a small army of action figures scattered across the floor, and colourful building blocks are piled high in one corner. Arvind, with his work as a cartoon artist, often brings home an endless stream of toys—Iron

Man, Hulk, Spiderman—each one seeming to multiply like magic. Priya loves that the kids are so happy with the gifts, but sometimes she wishes the toys would stay in their proper places... just for a little while.

When Arvind finally reaches his office, he calls Priya as he always does, just to check in.

"Hey, I've reached," Arvind says cheerfully into the phone. "What are you doing?"

Priya answers with a hint of playful exhaustion in her voice, looking around at the scattered toys. "Oh,... just cleaning up Hulks and Ironmans... again," she says, a laugh escaping her as she picks up a tiny Captain America, momentarily forgetting her frustration.

With the yelling from Nirav, the boys wake up from the sofas, and Arvind, who has been snoring while watching the news, is also startled. Baby Arya walks out of the room, rubbing sleep from her eyes, her little face still puffy from her nap. She's wearing a soft, faded pink onesie with tiny teddy bears on it, and her diaper peeks out from under the hem as she waddles in, probably wondering what has just happened.

"Yes!" Ishan says, pumping his fist in the air when he hears the news of not having to go to school for a week.

"Yes, no, yes—if you're not behaving well..." Priya says, her voice filled with anger, but she's suddenly interrupted by Niraj, who mockingly smiles and adds, "You'll leave us at your parents' house."

"No, I'll take Arya and go to my house. You guys do whatever you like," she retorts.

Niraj's smile disappears as he looks at his father.

"And now, shut up and have your lunch," Priya orders.

"We are the Avengers!" Niraj says, as the elder ones—Niraj and Nirav—play Captain America and Ironman. They assign Ishan as Spider-Man, though he doesn't seem to like it. If he doesn't agree, he'll be kicked out of the "Avengers" group. Little Arya is the Black Widow, even though most of the time, she's unaware of what's happening. She enjoys joining her brothers' "Avengers" party.

But the most interesting thing for the kids is Arvind's storytelling. He's an excellent storyteller, and the kids adore him. The only way to make them sit quietly is through his stories. That's how powerful his storytelling is. Priya isn't as much of a fan of his stories, but she encourages him because it gives her some free time.

"Smash!" The plates shatter as Niraj hits the ball into the plate section of the almirah inside the flat, while they are playing cricket later that night after dinner.

The sound echoes through the house. Priya rushes toward them from the other room. Her heart sinks as she sees the broken pieces scattered across the floor.

"Oh my god!" Arvind exclaims, trembling, as he has also been playing with the kids.

Priya's face flushes with anger. She stands frozen for a moment, her hands on her hips. "I've told you over and over not to play inside the house. What more can I say if the father is also with the kids?" she yells.

The room goes still. The kids look at each other, then at their parents, guilt written all over their faces.

"Who took the bat, Ishan?" Priya's voice is sharp now. "Haven't I hidden it?"

Ishaan hesitates. "Father gave it to us," he replies softly.

A flash of fury crosses Priya's face, and she takes a deep breath to steady herself. She can feel her anger rising, but she also knows the kids are just being... well, kids.

Arvind, sensing the tension, quickly steps in. "Don't worry, you take a rest. I'll clear it. Chill, chill!" He runs to grab a broom, trying to lighten the mood with his usual laid-back approach.

But Priya isn't done. She turns to the kids, who are still standing quietly, waiting for her to say something. "I shouldn't hear any sound from you guys anymore this week. Enough is enough. Go to your room."

The kids trudge off, heads down, each step heavier than the last.

Later, Priya checks on the kids.

She finds them sitting silently in their room, still avoiding eye contact. There is an awkward tension in the air, their once lively energy replaced by the weight of the broken plates.

"Haven't you slept yet?" Priya asks, her voice softer now, though still tinged with frustration.

They don't answer. They are lost in their own guilt, unsure of how to approach her.

"Okay," Priya says, sighing. "You've broken my plates, and now you're not talking to me either? Fine."

Before leaving, she turns to Arya, who is standing nearby, her little face scrunched in confusion. "Are you coming with me, or are you staying with your brothers?" Priya asks.

"Arya is not coming," Arya answers in her cute little voice, much to her mother's surprise.

Priya's lips twitch into a small smile, though it doesn't quite reach her eyes. "Don't come to me at midnight, then. I'm going to close my door," she says, her tone playful but weary. With that, she leaves the room.

The baby becomes a bit confused, watching her mother leave. Her little footsteps follow Priya's retreating figure, but she doesn't call out. Instead, she pauses for a moment, as though unsure of what has just happened.

A while later, Priya finds Arvind cleaning the broken plates, his expression focused and calm. Seeing him like this, her frustration from earlier begins to soften.

"Arvind, leave it," Priya says, sitting beside him, her voice quieter now. "I can manage it."

"No, no," he replies, shaking his head. "You carry on. I'll finish this and come."

She lets out a small laugh, but it is tinged with weariness. "Not that. The kids are in a sad mood and not talking to me. Only you can lighten the mood," she says. "Go ahead, I'll join later. The thing is, if the kids aren't in full swing, this week will be boring. I need them happy and lively—it makes everything better, for all of us."

Arvind smiles warmly, planting a gentle kiss on her forehead. "Don't worry, I can handle it. You go rest," he says, his voice reassuring. "I'll get them back in a good mood."

Arvind enters the kids' room a little while later; the room is dark except for the dim light from the hallway. He can see the boys sitting in bed, their faces reflecting the weight of the situation. They haven't fallen asleep yet.

"Hey, Avengers!" he says softly, sitting down beside them on the bed, trying to break the ice.

Niraj, still unsure, looks up. "Is mom still angry?"

Arvind nods as he settles next to them. "What we did is not permissible under mommy's rules, right? We broke her favorite plates. She definitely has a right to be angry."

The boys remain silent, their heads down.

He continues, his voice calm. "No issue. She's our mommy, right? We can make her happy. But promise me you'll apologize to her afterwards."

"Promise," they say in unison, their voices small but sincere.

"Okay, then. Good night, kids. Sleep well. Arya, are you coming?" Arvind asks as he stands up, preparing to leave the room.

They look at each other, but no one responds.

"What happened?" Arvind asks, noticing their silence

Ishaan speaks up first, his voice soft. "We're not sleepy, Dad."

Arvind raises an eyebrow, as if expecting something. "Oh?" he says, looking at them.

"So, can you tell us a story?" Niraj asks eagerly.

"It's already night, kids. I'll tell you one tomorrow for sure," Arvind replies, trying to wrap things up.

But the kids don't give up. "Please, Dad!" they all chime in, their voices full of pleading.

A smile tugs at Arvind's lips. He isn't about to leave just yet. Getting out of bed, Arya toddles over to him, reaching up to grab his hand. "Please, Dad, come," she says in her sweet, tiny voice.

Arvind chuckles softly and is gently pulled back to the bed, now surrounded by his kids. He can't resist.

"We're ready!" Ishaan exclaims, excitement in his eyes.

"Mm... which story do you want to hear?" Arvind asks, settling into the centre of the bed.

"Any story, Dad," Niraj replies, grinning.

"Let me think..." Arvind says, pretending to ponder. He pauses for a moment before his face lights up. "Yes, I've got one," he says, a smile spreading across his face.

Clearing his throat dramatically, Arvind begins, "In the heart of an enchanted forest..."

Chapter 2

"In the heart of an enchanted, vast forest, there lived many animals. The towering trees whispered secrets to the wind, while the air was thick with the scent of moss and earth. Sunlight filtered through the leaves, casting dappled shadows on the forest floor." Arvind's voice is soft, yet full of hidden excitement as he shares the story.

"Enchanted?" Niraj interrupts, his voice tinged with curiosity. "What do you mean by enchanted?"

Arvind pauses, smiling gently. He knows how these words always spark interest. "Yes, enchanted. This forest is special. Animals, birds, and humans can speak with one another here. It's said that there are jungle spirits watching over the land, though none have ever been seen."

The kids lean in, their eyes wide with wonder, as they imagine a world where every creature can speak.

"The forest is vast and full of life," Arvind continues. "Lions, tigers, wolves, elephants, giraffes—each one with a home there. Streams and small lakes dot the land, and trees stretch so high they seem to touch the sky. It's a perfect place for every animal to thrive. But, even here, there are moments of conflict—hunts, territorial battles—but for the most part, it's peaceful."

The children listen closely, lost in the imagery of the forest.

"Is this the story of the Lion, the King?" Ishaan asks eagerly, his voice bright with excitement.

Arvind's smile falters slightly, and he sighs. "No. And if you keep interrupting, I'll have to stop."

The room falls silent as the kids exchange guilty glances. They hold their breaths, eager for the story to continue.

"As I was saying," Arvind continues, his tone steady, "the forest was home to many different communities—wolf packs, lion prides, herds of elephants. The older animals, proud and set in their ways, believed their kind could solve their problems alone. But the young ones were different. They didn't care about old grudges. They played together, talked with each other. Their worlds weren't defined by the boundaries of species or history.

Rex, the wolf cub, and Zara, the lion cub, were at the centre of this change. They were unlikely friends, their bond stronger than the territories that divided their families. With them were Echo, the deer, Jumbo, the young elephant, and Max, Zara's older brother. They were inseparable, united by their adventures.

One evening, the sky turned soft shades of pink and orange as the sun began to set. The moon rose quietly, and the forest seemed to exhale in the cool air. The group played together, their laughter echoing through the clearing.

"Let's play again!" Rex shouted, bouncing on his paws.

"I'm done for today," Jumbo said with a yawn, stretching his massive yet small legs. "My mom's probably looking for me."

"I'm leaving too," Max added, flicking his tail. "Zara, don't be late. Father will want to know where you are."

"We're heading back as well," the others said, slowly wandering off, leaving only Echo, Rex, and Zara behind.

"Okay, are we playing or what?" Echo asked, a hint of disappointment in her voice.

"Yes, we can play," Rex replied, his excitement returning. "The game's simple. You run and hide, and Zara and I will try to catch you. The one who catches you first wins."

"Heh, that'll be easy," Zara said, a cocky smirk on his face. "We've been hunting deer all our lives."

Echo grinned. "...and we always outrun you guys!"

"Alright, alright, enough talk," Rex interrupted with a laugh. "Let's just play."

"I'm the next king, and you'll see why," Zara said, puffing out his chest proudly.

And just like that, the game was on.

Echo darted away first, her slender legs carrying her quickly through the trees. Zara was quick to follow, muscles rippling as he sprinted with ease, tail flicking with determination. He was so sure of himself, his eyes locked on the trail Echo left behind.

But Rex—Rex had other plans.

Realizing he couldn't keep up in terms of speed or strength, Rex did what he did best: think. With a quick glance, he spotted a sturdy tree and scaled it swiftly, gaining a higher vantage point. From up here, he could see much further, and his eyes scanned the forest for any sign of Echo.

Zara was focused on the chase, but Rex knew the real challenge wasn't in who was faster—it was in who could outsmart the game.

Meanwhile, Echo had decided to venture deeper into the forest, putting distance between herself and her pursuers. She ran, her hooves light against the forest floor, but after a while, she slowed, her breath coming quicker. Her muscles ached from the chase, and she needed to rest.

She crouched behind a bush, her sides heaving as she tried to catch her breath. Her eyes, though, kept darting to a large rock nearby. It looked... strange. The rock shifted, ever so slightly, as though something beneath it was moving. Echo's pulse quickened.

Crkk!

A loud crack shattered the stillness. It was Rex. He had misjudged his landing and crashed into the rock, breaking the tree bark above him. Echo snapped out of her thoughts, startled by the sound.

"Ha! Caught you!" Rex shouted triumphantly, though his voice trailed off as he saw Echo's wide, frightened eyes.

She wasn't looking at him. She was staring at the rock, and her unease was growing with every passing second.

Before Rex could fully comprehend what was happening, a sudden shift in the ground caught Echo's eye. Her heart skipped a beat as she instinctively jumped back in fear. Beneath Rex, the earth trembled, and what Echo had mistaken for a rock now revealed itself to be an enormous, ancient bear. Rex had unknowingly stepped right on top of the creature, rousing it from its slumber.

The bear let out a deafening roar, its teeth sharp and exposed in a vicious snarl. The sound rumbled through the forest, heavy and terrifying, sending a cold shiver down their spines and making the very ground beneath them seem to tremble.

The air felt thick, oppressive, as if the entire forest held its breath. Rex and Echo, both startled by the sudden threat, didn't hesitate for a second. They turned and ran, their hearts racing, adrenaline pumping through their veins. The bear's roar echoed in their ears as they darted between the trees, the weight of fear pressing down on them.

Finally, after what felt like an eternity, the sounds of the bear faded. The forest around them seemed to quiet, almost as if it had exhaled. They slowed their pace, panting heavily, their bodies trembling from the exertion.

"That was too close," Rex muttered, wiping sweat from his brow.

Echo's voice was shaky. "Who... Who was that?"

"That," Rex said, still catching his breath, "was Thorne, the old bear of the jungle."

"He's so huge," Echo said, awestruck. "He must be ancient."

"Yeah," Rex agreed. "He's as old as the tallest trees in this forest. He's been here longer than anyone, and while he doesn't hunt anymore—probably because of his age—his presence is enough to scare everyone. My mom says he likes kids, but I've never really seen it. His actions are different from what she says."

As they calmed down, the weight of the situation hit them. Suddenly, Echo stopped dead in her tracks.

"Rex," she whispered, her voice trembling, "Where's Zara?"

Rex froze, his eyes scanning the woods. Zara was nowhere to be seen.

"He's probably still looking for you," Rex said, trying to reassure her, though doubt crept into his voice.

The forest grew quieter as Rex and Echo began to search for Zara. The sky had darkened, and shadows stretched long across the ground, making the trees seem even taller and more imposing.

They moved carefully, their steps soft against the forest floor, trying not to disturb the quiet. Rex's heart pounded in his chest, his thoughts racing as he scanned the trees, hoping for any sign of his friend. The night was growing darker, and a sense of urgency pushed them forward. They decided to check the lion's territory, wondering if Zara might have already returned home.

As they neared the lion's domain, the forest seemed to shift. The trees grew thicker, their branches reaching higher, and the air was heavy with the scent of the lion pride. It was a place of power, where the ruling family lived, and it was not a place children like them wandered without fear. No one dared approach this land lightly, especially not without cause.

Ahead, they saw the grand podium, where King Leo would sit when addressing the animals of the jungle. It had been many years since anyone had gathered there, yet the spot still radiated an undeniable authority, as if the echoes of past meetings still hung in the air. This was the sacred ground where only the king and his family were meant to stand—no one else dared to set foot in there."

"Is the podium just like in *The Lion King*?" Ishaan asks, his voice curious.

"Exactly, dear," Arvind says, "just like how Simba and his father sit there. Here, Zara, his brother Max, and their father, Leo, the fierce king, would rest."

"Is Zara there?" Niraj asks, his eyes wide, as if the whole jungle might be hiding within the shadows.

"Rex and Echo cautiously scanned the area from a distance. But there was no sign of Zara. Only Leo, the great king of the jungle, sat there, his massive form illuminated by the pale moonlight. His eyes flickered in their direction, but his gaze was distant, lost in thought.

Rex felt a knot form in his stomach. He had hoped to find Zara there, but there was no sign of him.

The weight of the situation pressed down on Rex. His fur bristled, and a tightness crept into his limbs as his mind raced with worry. They had to find Zara. There was no way they could leave things this way, uncertain and unresolved. As the tension swelled within him, Rex knew he needed help—someone who could guide him, someone who could understand. So, he decided to share his growing concern with his family, hoping they would come to his aid.

His heart pounded in his chest as he approached his mother, Luna. Her calm presence was both a comfort and a reminder that he wasn't quite ready for the responsibility he was feeling.

"That's not our business, son," Luna, his mother, said, her voice calm but firm. "The lions can handle it themselves."

"But he's my friend!" Rex protested, his voice tinged with frustration.

"They can solve their own issues, Rex," Luna responded, her tone hardening. "There's no point in us getting involved. And they won't appreciate it. We don't like interfering too." Her words held the weight of finality, leaving no room for argument.

Rex felt a sharp pang in his chest. Was he really just supposed to let it go? The thought of Zara, out there alone and vulnerable, made his stomach twist. "But I can't just leave him," he said softly, almost to himself. The silence that followed felt heavy.

But Rex's heart refused to give up. He couldn't abandon Zara like that. "Please, can't we talk to Dad? Maybe he can help."

Luna shook her head, her expression inscrutable. "I can't, and he won't," she said firmly. "It's time for the hunt, Rex. Come join us. Your brothers are ready. You're in the middle today. Keep an eye on your sisters up front. Pappa will be at the back."

Rex felt the words like a weight pressing on his chest. But he couldn't just drop it. "I won't come. I'm going to find him!" Rex shouted, his frustration finally spilling over. Without waiting for any response, he turned and dashed off, his paws pounding the earth.

Luna's gaze followed him, her face softening for just a moment. "Rex... Rex! Come back!" she called, her voice laced with concern, but her son didn't stop. His figure grew smaller, disappearing into the distance.

Luna let out a frustrated sigh, muttering something under her breath as she turned toward her mate, Drake. The alpha wolf stood tall, a force of nature, his amber eyes sharp with an unyielding intensity. His muscles rippled with power as he surveyed the pack, his presence commanding and unwavering.

"What happened?" Drake asked, his voice steady, betraying no hint of emotion.

"Nothing, just these kids," Luna replied, her tone tight and irritated.

Drake stared at her for a moment, sensing there was more. Luna finally sighed and added, "Actually, Rex's friend Zara, the lion, is missing. He's asking for our help to find her."

"Mmm," Drake grunted in response, his face revealing no expression. He turned without another word and walked away, the matter seemingly dismissed.

Luna watched Rex disappear further into the forest, her heart heavy. The jungle was vast and full of dangers, and Rex was just a cub, brimming with determination but not yet prepared for what lay ahead. She wished he could see the wisdom in waiting, but she knew his heart too well. Once it was set on something, nothing would stop him.

Later, with no help from his family or any of his friends' families, Rex stood at a crossroads. The world around him seemed to stretch infinitely, and he couldn't bear the thought of inaction any longer. He had to find Zara. If that meant stepping into the unknown, into the lion's territory, then so be it. He would find a way, even if it was just him against everything the jungle could throw at him.

The others had tried to dissuade him. Echo, the deer; Jumbo, the young elephant; all of them had begged him to be patient, to wait for a better moment. But Rex felt that moment slipping away, each minute more precious than the last. And so, his resolve hardened.

Rex squared his shoulders, pushing through the gnawing anxiety as he made his way toward the lion's territory. The air grew colder, and the familiar woods felt different, more oppressive. The trees seemed to crowd in around him, and the shadows stretched unnervingly long. The wind whispered through the leaves, but Rex couldn't make sense of the sounds.

His small paws felt lighter with each step, though a knot tightened in his chest. The moon barely broke through the dense canopy, casting faint shadows on the ground. The familiar landmarks seemed distant now, as if the forest had changed with the very thought of entering the lion's domain.

It was a place filled with power, something Rex couldn't ignore. He was just a small wolf cub, alone in a world far bigger than he ever imagined. Each step felt heavier, his uncertainty growing as he neared the unknown.

Although Rex tried to project confidence for his friends, deep down, fear gnawed at him. This was his first time stepping into the lion's territory, and his heart raced with every step into the unknown.

He searched the area for Leo, the King, scanning the surroundings carefully. Every rustling leaf or shift in the shadows made him hopeful, but the mighty lion was nowhere in sight. As his gaze drifted across the space, something caught his attention. The podium where the kings of the jungle had stood. He'd always wondered what it would be like to stand there, to be in the place of such power.

Without a second thought, Rex climbed up and stood tall, his paws settling into the spot where the rulers had once addressed the jungle.

"What a view!" he reflected, his voice barely a whisper, as if speaking to the entire jungle.

"Citizens of the kingdom, great and small..." Rex half-jokingly mimicked the words he had heard from his mother, Luna. She had once told him stories of the old days when King Lothar, Leo's father, had addressed the jungle when a massive wildfire struck. The king's words had soothed the forest, and Luna had never quite shaken the fear in her eyes when recalling that incident. Rex had always felt that that wildfire had left an indelible mark on his mother, one she never spoke of directly, but which lingered in her gaze.

The soft rustle of the leaves whispered in the background, and Rex felt the weight of his surroundings grow heavier. Something about being on the podium felt different. A strange unease settled into his chest, as if the jungle itself were holding its breath.

Suddenly, a thunderous voice roared from behind him.

"Who's that?!"

Rex froze in fear.

The massive lion approached him, anger burning in his eyes. "How dare you stand here on my podium?" King Leo's voice boomed, his fur rippling with fury.

Rex's heart raced as he backed away, almost falling from the podium. His eyes filled with fear and sadness, searching for a way out.

"Dad... No! No!" Young Max, Zara's brother, swiftly approached his father Leo and stopped just short of him. He stepped forward in defence of his friend.

"Hey, why did you come here?" Max demanded, his voice sharp.

Rex was so frightened he couldn't find the words to reply.

"Dad, let him go," Max urged, his voice quieter now but firm.

Leo, sensing his son's interruption, slowly turned, giving Max a cold, unwavering stare. His movements were deliberate, as if he were deciding whether to allow this to continue.

Max, feeling the pressure, turned back to Rex. "You go now," he said, his tone laced with a forced calm, trying to mask the tension growing between the two.

Rex swallowed hard, his thoughts racing. "I want to talk to you about one thing," he said, voice trembling slightly.

"Rex, not this time. We have a problem," Max replied, his eyes flickering to his father, gauging the situation.

Leo stopped in his tracks, his massive form blocking the path, then slowly turned his head to look back at his son, Max. The jungle seemed to grow still in that moment, as if everything was waiting to see what would happen next.

Max's voice lowered, the tension hanging thick in the air. "Dad... Zara is missing."

Rex's heart sank as he caught Max's words. He immediately bowed his head to Leo in respect and said, "Your Grace, I came to speak of the same news. Zara was playing with us, and then he was gone. We searched, but couldn't find him."

Leo's eyes widened slightly, and for a moment, the weight of the news seemed to settle heavily on him. His usual commanding presence faltered, just for an instant, as the gravity of Zara's disappearance hit him. His silence spoke volumes, the jungle holding its breath along with him.

At that moment, King Leo's sharp gaze turned skyward, and he saw Rook, the eagle approaching. Apart from the lion community, Leo only truly acknowledged one other creature—the wise eagle, Rook, his most trusted companion. Straightforward and deadly, much like the rook in chess, Rook flew high above the jungle, always vigilant. His keen eyes saw what others could not, and his loyalty to Leo was unwavering.

Rook descended gracefully and landed nearby. There was a brief silence. Leo's attention sharpened. The jungle seemed to stand still around them.

Rook stood tall, his gaze steady as he spoke. "Your Grace..." he began, his voice measured, every word carrying weight.

Leo's ears twitched, and every eye was on Rook. Everyone in the vicinity knew that when Rook spoke, it was not without reason.

"I have news," Rook continued, and the words seemed to hang in the air.

The jungle fell into an even deeper silence.

"The humans have begun camping on the edge of our jungle. I've seen many of them moving around, and it doesn't feel right." Rook's eyes darkened as he spoke, his usual calm demeanour edged with an unfamiliar sense of urgency. "I have also seen Vexor, the tiger, with them. We must be cautious—this could mean trouble for us all."

The words hit Leo like a physical blow. A tightening in his chest made it hard to breathe. The weight of Rook's warning collided with his growing panic over Zara's disappearance.

Leo's thoughts swirled. The unease about the humans, coupled with the growing fear for Zara's safety, pressed heavily on his mind. Something was wrong—deeply wrong—and Leo could feel it in his very bones.

A cold shiver ran down his spine, but his regal composure remained. Yet, the tightening in his chest, the pounding of his heart—he knew something was coming, but he didn't know what it was."

Chapter 3

"Let me drink some water, and I'll be right back," Arvind says as he walks out of the room, needing a brief break from the intense narration. Little Arya follows her father, her tiny footsteps echoing in the quiet house.

Meanwhile, the toys are back in the kids' hands. Ishan, deep into his play, growls as he manipulates the Hulk action figure. "Thorne is my Hulk—he's huge. Grrrr," he says, acting out Hulk's strength.

"Who was Thorne, by the way?" Niraj asks Nirav.

"The bear, idiot," Nirav teases with a smirk.

Ishan, as usual, interrupts. "At the end, Avengers will come to save the animals."

Nirav sighs, clearly frustrated. "This isn't your endgame..." He rolls his eyes, tired of Ishan's constant excitement, as if he is far too old to be indulging in such childish fantasies. "These kids..."

The conversations continue in their usual playful tone until Priya and Arvind, with Arya in his arms, walk back into the room. The kids immediately fall silent. The tension from earlier that night—plates smashing, their mother's sharp words—hangs in the air, a palpable reminder of what has just happened.

Priya, raising an eyebrow, asks, "Why are you all up after 11 pm?"

"Maa... please... we don't have classes tomorrow," Nirav protests, his voice hopeful.

Arvind shoots a quick look at the kids, silently signalling them to apologize for their earlier behaviour.

"What happened?" Priya asks, her tone still stern but softening a little.

"They're sorry for what happened," Arvind says quietly.

Priya smiles, though it doesn't quite reach her eyes. "Oh, don't say that. I know my boys." Her smile, faint but reassuring, makes the boys relax a little.

"Can we hear the rest of the story?" Ishan asks eagerly, the tension lifting slightly.

Priya glances at Arvind before replying. "Actually, the one-week curfew might be reduced soon."

Arvind's eyes narrow. "Why? What happened?"

Priya continues, "A youth association took the issue to court. They're claiming the government sponsors these communal riots to hijack elections. The court's siding with them for now."

"That's good to hear," Arvind replies, nodding thoughtfully.

"So, does that mean we should go to school tomorrow?" Nirav asks, his voice tinged with worry.

"I didn't finish my homework," Niraj mutters.

"No, it's not about school," Priya says. "The curfew might be shortened, that's all."

Ishan, with his typical enthusiasm, pushes forward. "So, can we hear the rest of the story now?"

"Come on, Mom, sit with us," Nirav urges, pulling at her hand.

Priya sighs but gives in, sitting down with Arya on her lap. The room settles into a more comfortable silence as Arvind resumes his story.

Arvind's voice grows serious, reflecting the change in tone of the story he is about to tell.

"As things started to get tense," he begins, "King Leo ordered Rook, the eagle, to report back on human movements. Rook flew to the outskirts of the jungle, hoping to uncover their plans. But what he didn't know was that Rex, the young wolf, was also spying on the humans at the same time. Rex, loyal to Zara, had been tracking the humans for a while, and now, more than ever, he knew he had to protect him."

Arvind pauses, letting the tension settle in the room. The children listen intently.

"Hidden high in the branches of a thick tree, Rook remained motionless, his sharp eyes scanning the camp below. The humans were unaware of his presence—his dark feathers blended perfectly with the leaves. Below him, Rex crouched low in the underbrush, his gaze fixed on the camp. Neither animal knew the other was there, both intent on the same target.

The camp was not small—there were around 10 to 15 humans, all wearing camouflage uniforms. The air seemed charged with intent as they moved between tables cluttered with maps, charts, and various plans pinned to makeshift boards. Rook could hear fragments of their low murmurs but struggled to piece together the full conversation from the distance.

His talons gripped the tree bark tightly as he inched forward, trying to get closer without being noticed. His heart raced—he was so close to uncovering something important.

One of the humans spoke louder, and Rook froze, his attention sharp. His feathers rustled ever so slightly as he shifted, hoping to catch the full meaning of their words. He couldn't afford to miss anything now. The future of the jungle, of Zara, depended on what these humans were planning.

Then, the leader of the group, a man in his mid-50s, stepped forward. His brown hair was greying at the temples and his bulky physique made him look imposing despite his age. His name was Robert.

"Finally," Robert said, his voice gravelly with anticipation, "our efforts are going to be noticed. The animals are starting to realize the threat. We need that fear in their eyes. Years ago, my great-grandfather and his team camped here, plotted their plan, and set the wildfire to threaten the animals, to make them submit to our control. Somehow the animals managed to escape, but it was a start. Then, another team cut down the trees to send a warning, but the animals didn't react. They didn't care. But now... now, with the kidnapping of Zara, we've finally hit the mark. The future king of the jungle. And we will use that fear to control them."

Laughter echoed through the camp, low and chilling. Robert continued, his hands tapping the bench in front of him for emphasis. "Yes, yes... this is just the beginning."

At that moment, a figure appeared, dragging Zara—the lion cub—his body chained and visibly exhausted. His paws dragged the ground, and his golden eyes, once bright and proud, now seemed dull with fear and exhaustion. His head hung low, as if defeated, each step a struggle. The chains clinked with every movement.

Robert's cold gaze followed the procession as Zara was thrust before him, his voice cutting through the silence. "This is the sign we needed. The jungle is under our control. We don't wish to destroy it—but we will take its power." He paused, letting his words settle like poison in the air. "To gain that power, we will need to make some sacrifices. We must kill if needed, to stir fear. They must believe we control their future. They must understand that everything we do is for their benefit. For their survival."

The group responded with an eerie, unified agreement, their hands tapping rhythmically on the wooden benches. The sound reverberated like a dark hymn.

Robert turned away from Zara, his eyes scanning the group. "Take him back," he ordered flatly, waving his hand dismissively. As two men moved to pull Zara away, Robert's gaze grew sharp, his voice low and compelling. "But there's another we must acknowledge. Another ally who will make us unstoppable. Vexor!"

The camp fell silent as a figure emerged from the shadows—a massive tiger, his every step purposeful and commanding. The grace and power of his movements spoke volumes, but there was something unsettling in his eyes. He was not part of the jungle's natural order, but a force crafted by necessity.

He stepped into the clearing, and the group clapped in approval, a cold and mechanical sound that echoed through the camp.

"Vexor," Robert continued, his tone smooth, "has been cast out by his own kind. A lone tiger, rejected, wandering until I found him. He will stand beside us, and we will crown him king. Together, we will rule this jungle."

The men clapped again, the sound reverberating through the air with a sickly resonance.

Vexor spoke, his voice low and deliberate. "I will fulfil my word. I will bring the animals to you. They will follow me—or they will follow you. Either way, they will serve."

Robert's smile was thin, almost imperceptible, but his approval was clear. "That's the spirit of a king," he said. "Now, go and prepare. Build your army. Gather those who will fight by your side."

Vexor nodded once, his eyes lingering on Robert before he turned and disappeared back into the shadows of the jungle.

Robert stood still for a moment, his eyes scanning the camp. Then, with a purposeful stride, he walked to a large chalkboard. He reached for the duster and wiped away what had been written earlier:

Task 1: Giving a shock: Kidnap member of king's family.

Once the board was cleared, he took a piece of chalk and, with deliberate motion, wrote:

Task 2: Studying the Animals.

He paused, turning back to the group, his voice now cutting through the quiet. "Before we take control, we must understand the jungle and the animals who will resist us. We must learn their ways. We will start with the wolves—cunning, fierce, and highly organized. They hunt in packs—stronger together than apart. The dominant pair leads the pack, but there are as many as thirty-six wolves in a single pack. So, the idea is to never face them alone. Never. If you hear howling, understand they are sending a signal. That is when we are in trouble."

The group listened intently, the air thick with tension, and Robert's words hung heavily in the space between them.

"Any questions?" Robert's voice sliced through the still air as he glanced over the group, his tone sharp and commanding.

A man from the front row raised his hand, his face tense with curiosity. "Robert, what about the king of the jungle and his family?"

Robert's eyes flickered, a cold smile playing at the corners of his lips. He leaned forward, his voice carrying the weight of cold, calculated intent. "Let the king rule for now," he said slowly, letting his words sink in. "But let's see how much power he holds when his people are under threat. We'll make him witness as his kin are destroyed, stripped away from him. We will isolate him—make him alone."

A low, dark laugh rippled through the group, like a shared secret of cruelty.

"First, we break the others," Robert continued, his voice steady, unwavering. "Then, when he's the last one standing, we take him down. Alone. Vulnerable."

The others nodded, their agreement silent but understood.

Robert's voice grew more intense as he addressed the group, his gaze scanning each person with a calm, yet unnerving precision. "Now, let me tell you about another interesting creature—the bear."

He paused, letting the words settle before continuing. "What makes bears unique is that they can walk on two legs, just like humans, and on all fours, like any other animal. Their strength... is unmatched. If we ever come face to face with one in the wild, it's the end of us. They can tear us apart with a single swipe."

The group exchanged uneasy glances, the weight of his words sinking in. They all knew the power of the beast that Robert was referring to, their imaginations running wild with the idea of facing such a creature.

"But," Robert's tone shifted, an edge of dark amusement creeping into his voice, "fortunately, the jungle has only one bear. And it's old—too old to even stand up properly. So, it's not much of a threat to us. But you might be wondering why I bring it up now."

He took a deliberate step forward, his eyes locking with the man who had asked about the lion earlier. "Gentlemen, I introduce you to our new chemically engineered bear. Prime-9."

As Robert spoke, a shadow loomed over the group. A low growl rumbled through the air, sending a chill down their spines. A massive, hulking bear, its eyes glowing with an unnatural ferocity. Its size was imposing, its muscles rippling under its thick fur, making the ground tremble with every step it took.

The men froze, their faces a mixture of awe and fear as Prime-9 stepped into the clearing, its presence undeniable. It was a force of nature, a twisted creation far beyond the wildest creatures of the jungle.

Robert's voice cut through the tension, sharp and commanding. "This... this will be our trump card against your king and his family," he said, nodding toward the man who had spoken earlier. "This is the weapon that will tear down their defences and force them to submit. No animal stands a chance against this."

Robert motioned for Prime-9 to be sent back into the shadows of the jungle. The massive bear retreated, leaving behind a sense of unease that hung in the air like a storm waiting to break.

At that moment, one of Robert's colleagues spoke up, curiosity mixed with caution. "What exactly does this chemically engineered thing do, Robert?"

Robert turned, his expression hardening as he prepared to explain. "Prime-9 was captured from another jungle a few years ago," he began. "We've trained him to be stronger, specifically to fight against the animals here and fight for us. We've chemically enhanced him, making him more vicious, more ferocious, more ruthless. He's been engineered to be unempathetic, to have no feelings for his own kind. He will tear through these animals without hesitation."

He paused, letting the weight of his words settle on the group. The men listened intently, eyes widening at the sheer coldness of it all.

"Additionally, since he's from another jungle," Robert continued, "he doesn't have the same connections to these animals. No bonds, no loyalty. He will tear through them without hesitation—no questions, no remorse. And our chemicals will ensure that."

There was a moment of silence before Robert's tone grew sharper. "We can't fully trust that tiger, Vexor. He's still from their group. He might change his mind, and he might be manipulated. So, Prime-9 is our true trump card. He's our sure thing."

As the full weight of his words settled in, a sense of awe and unease washed over the group. Robert's colleagues exchanged glances, impressed by the lengths they had gone to secure control of the jungle.

The tapping on the benches started again, rhythmic and almost hypnotic, the men acknowledging Robert's words, each beat amplifying the cold excitement in the air. It was clear that Prime-9 would be the weapon that would solidify their dominance over the jungle.

Another person raised his hand, a question on his mind. "Robert, we've made plans for the wolves, we've dealt with the lions, we have an engineered bear, and we have tigers on our side. But what about elephants? Those giants? They live in groups too, don't they?"

Robert chuckled, his amusement obvious. "The elephant group is matriarchal in nature," he said, smirking. "What can these bunch of ladies do?" His laughter echoed through the camp, drawing a few chuckles from the others.

He paused, letting the weight of his words settle before continuing. "Okay, let's say they come after us. What then? The maximum they can run is 100 meters. After that, they're out of breath. I'm in my 50s, and I can deal with them easily." He leaned back, his tone dismissive. "So, elephants are not a threat. Don't even consider them."

The others looked at each other and laughed in agreement, the tension easing. Robert's smile widened. "But," he added with a sly grin, "we will need them for loading and unloading things in the future."

The group burst into laughter again, the sound filling the air with a sense of false bravado.

"So, gentlemen, this is the plan," Robert began, his voice steady, cold. "We will attack and capture the jungle, dealing with each of the animals one by one. Once we've neutralized these groups, this jungle will be eighty percent under our control. We need this place, for our future generation, for our expansion."

His colleagues nodded in agreement, their voices rising, chanting, "Yes, yes!" in loud, unified approval.

"But before we move forward, there's one more little fellow we need to deal with," Robert added with a sly grin.

A moment of silence fell over the group. Confusion spread across their faces.

Without warning, Robert grabbed a slingshot from the table, loading it with a stone. He aimed and fired it with precision, sending it hurtling through the window with a sharp crack. The stone struck Rook, the eagle, who had been perched nearby, listening in from the trees. Rook had been unaware that he was so clearly visible to Robert. He hadn't anticipated being noticed or attacked. All this time, he thought he was safely hidden. But Robert had let him overhear, maybe on purpose, to make sure the jungle would become aware of what was coming—to fuel the fear, to make them obedient.

Rook faltered, and the stone hit him, sending him tumbling down, injured by the strike.

Rex, the young wolf, had been nearby and saw what happened. In a swift move, he rushed forward and helped Rook, who was struggling to stay airborne. Despite the pain, Rook managed to regain flight and fly away, though still wounded. Rex, realizing the danger, bolted with fear and ran into the jungle to escape, but Rook was out of immediate harm's way.

The group burst into laughter at the turn of events.

"For our future!" Robert yelled, his voice thick with satisfaction.

"FOR OUR FUTURE!" his colleagues echoed back, their voices rising in unison.

"Long live humans," Robert declared, a chilling grin spreading across his face.

"Long live humans!" the others repeated, their voices dripping with dangerous fervour."

Chapter 4

"Actually, what really happened to Zara?" Priya asks, her voice soft yet filled with curiosity.

"Hey, what Amma?" Nirav responds, sounding disappointed.

"Amma wasn't present right at the start of the story, that's why. I don't know... can you tell me?" Priya says, her expression pleading for answers.

Ishan stands up abruptly. "Amma, I will tell you," he says, his voice steady but with a hint of urgency.

"Zara is the son of Leo, the king lion. Rex, the wolf cub, Echo, the deer, Jumbo, the young elephant... they are friends. One day, while they were playing, Zara, the lion cub went missing. Rex took the responsibility of finding him, but after he failed he reported to King Leo and Max, Zara's brother. And after that, you know what happened, right?"

"Yes, yes, I understood now. Thanks, dear," Priya says.

"Amma, I will say another thing also," Nirav says, his eyes gleaming excitedly.

"What's that?" Priya asks, intrigued.

"Zara is Loki, and Rex is Thor. In the end, Rex will come and help him from capture," Nirav says with a sense of finality.

Priya's face scrunches up in confusion. "Who are these Loki and Thor?" she asks, glancing at Aravind.

Arvind's face darkens, his patience thinning. "If you guys are interrupting again with your Marvel characters and confusing things, I'm stopping the narration."

"No, no! Sorry, sorry!" Niraj apologizes immediately, turning to his siblings with a warning. "Let's not bring these references again."

Arya, in her sweet little voice, asks, "Papa, what happened afterwards in our forest? Did humans capture it?"

Aravind's tone softens as he resumes the story.

"The news and findings from Rook, the eagle, who had been eavesdropping on the human camp, spread quickly through the jungle. Soon, a family meeting was called in the lion's den. Only the immediate family gathered, with Rook, the eagle, present to share his findings. The tension in the air was palpable as they awaited further instructions.

"I need my son, right now!" Zara's mother cried, her voice quivering with despair. "You can stay here and make plans, but I'm going to get him back myself!" Tears welled up in her eyes as the pain of the moment overwhelmed her.

"Don't overreact," one of the lions interjected calmly. "We can't make rash decisions. We need to plan carefully before we strike."

"Overreact?" Zara's mother's voice broke with emotion. "I've lost my son to those heartless humans, and you think I'm overreacting?" She fought to control her sobs, the weight of her words pressing heavily in the air.

"Mom, that's not what he meant," Max said gently, stepping forward to console her. "We will bring Zara back, no matter what. But we have to plan carefully, or we risk putting ourselves in danger." His voice was steady, offering her a sense of reassurance.

Rook, the eagle, nodded in agreement. "Max is right. We need to strategize before attacking. These humans are not to be underestimated. I suggest we reach out to other animals for help, so we can be as strong as possible when the time comes."

"Yes, Dad," Max said to the king, his voice resolute. "Rex and my friends are already outside, ready to help us. But we have to be willing to take their help."

Leo, the king, rose from his perch, slowly walking toward the summit where only the king could stand. His voice echoed with authority.

"Whenever the forest is under threat, we lions are strong enough to face it. We've faced this before, and we will face it again—without anyone's help. This is our family matter, and the humans have openly challenged me and my family. We will respond accordingly. Do you understand?"

His words carried not only the weight of a leader's command but also the pride of the lions, unwilling to involve any other animal group in their struggle. It was a deep-seated belief, ingrained in the very essence of their family, that they alone could handle their battles. To ask for help was to admit weakness, and Leo, proud as he was, would never show that vulnerability.

Max, though silent, didn't agree with his father's dismissive attitude toward asking for help.

Rook, sensing the tension in the air and aware that Max hadn't replied, spoke up to avoid further conflict. "Yes, your grace," he said, his tone respectful, though laced with the subtle discomfort of the moment.

Leo's voice became cold and commanding. "Max, you will go and gather more information about the humans. I want to know their exact positions. We will strike soon and bring back Zara."

Max nodded solemnly and left.

Following King Leo's orders, Max set out to gather more intelligence about the humans' actions. Despite his father's refusal to seek help from others, Max knew he couldn't tackle this alone. He decided to take Zara's close friends, Rex the wolf and Jumbo the elephant, with him. Rex, eager and determined, was especially driven to find Zara and bring him back. His loyalty to his friend was unwavering, and he was ready to do whatever it took to help. Together, Max, Rex, and Jumbo moved through the jungle, quietly observing and searching for any signs of human activity.

Max, Rex, and Jumbo moved through the jungle, quietly searching for any signs of human presence.

"How is this a family matter?" Max muttered in frustration as he and his friends trekked through the jungle.

"I don't understand either," Jumbo said, shaking his head. "My parents said the same thing, and they didn't want to interfere in the fight against the humans."

"What same thing? How is it a family matter to you?" Rex asked, his brow furrowing.

"It's not like that," Jumbo explained, his voice heavy. "I asked my parents to help Leo, to stand with the lions and fight, but they said it wasn't their fight. They didn't want to take up arms against humans."

Rex sighed. "It's the same with my family. It feels like no one wants to take a stand, even with what's happening."

Max was shaking his head in disbelief. "How ridiculous is that? After everything Rook and Rex have seen, how can anyone think this is just about the lions?"

They continued walking, sharing their disbelief and frustration. They vented about the others who still didn't understand the severity of the situation. The blame was thrown around carelessly, each of them questioning how anyone could ignore the bigger picture. The deeper they walked into the forest, the heavier the silence grew, their words hanging in the air.

Suddenly, Rex stopped and motioned for the others to be quiet.

"Hey, wait, listen carefully," he said, his voice barely above a whisper.

Max and Rook froze, eyes narrowing as they strained to hear. Footsteps. Soft but steady. And they were getting closer.

It was Echo, the deer, and her family, walking toward them.

"Hey, Echo," Jumbo greeted. "Where are you all going now?" he asked, seeing the sadness in their eyes.

Echo looked down, unable to answer. Her mother spoke instead, "We're moving, Jumbo." Jumbo stood frozen, shocked and numb at the words.

"Moving?" Rex asked, confused.

"What do you mean, moving?" Max asked, his brow furrowed.

Echo's father spoke, his voice weary. "How can we stay here anymore, knowing what's coming? We're moving to a nearby jungle, somewhere safer."

Rex, frustrated, spoke up. "Yes, we're under threat, but how is leaving our home the answer? This is where we live. They're intruding, so why leave? Why not fight?"

Echo's father turned to Rex, his eyes sharp. "Listen, kid, we're under attack. You want us to stay here and risk dying at their hands? Is that what you'd want for your family? Or is it wiser to move somewhere safe and live freely?"

"We can make this a better place again, uncle," Rex pleaded. "We can help each other, unite, and fight the humans. We'll take our home back together! We'll fight them. The lions, wolves, elephants, everyone will be with us! We can do this together!"

"Really? Lions? The king can't even protect his child. He is going to protect us? Along with you children, you will also give protection?" Echo's father's voice was bitter, full of doubt and frustration.

Rex was silent, struggling to find the right words. His usual confidence had faltered in the face of Echo's father's harsh question. His voice barely came out as he turned to Echo one last time. "Hey Echo, please... don't go. Don't leave us. We'll fight, we'll protect each other... please stay."

Echo, her eyes brimming with tears, couldn't speak. She stood there, trembling, unable to offer Rex any words of comfort. The weight of her father's decision had silenced her. She looked at her friends, but couldn't meet their eyes. Her pain was too much to bear.

Max, sensing Rex's desperation, intervened softly. "Let them go, Rex. They've already made their decision. We can't change that."

Rex stood frozen, his heart sinking. Jumbo, standing beside him, was also struggling to keep his composure. Tears welled in his eyes as he looked at Echo one last time, knowing this might truly be their last moment together. The sorrow was overwhelming, and neither of them could say a word.

Echo, with one final tearful look at her friends, ran to Jumbo. Without a word, she threw herself into his arms, her embrace tight and full of unspoken grief. The farewell was too painful, too final, and even Echo's father couldn't stand to watch the moment unfold. He turned away, his own heart heavy with the impossible decision he had made.

"Let's go, Echo," he said quietly, his voice laced with regret, and began to lead the family away.

Echo pulled away from Jumbo, giving him one last, heart-wrenching hug. They held on to each other for a moment longer, knowing it was goodbye. With a final glance at her friends, Echo turned and followed her family into the depths of the forest.

Max, Rex, and Jumbo stood there, their hearts heavy with sadness. The jungle around them felt so much emptier now. Rex had tried to change her mind, but in the end, it hadn't mattered. Echo and her family were leaving, and nothing they said could stop it.

As they watched Echo's family disappear into the distance, the weight of the moment pressed down on them. The future of their home, their friendship, and everything they held dear was uncertain. The jungle would never be the same again.

"We have to go," Max said quietly after a long silence, the weight of what had just happened sinking in. He turned to look at his friends, but Jumbo was still in tears, his body trembling with the loss of Echo.

Rex, trying to stay strong for his companions, placed a paw on Jumbo's shoulder. "Jumbo, whatever happens, we always move on, buddy. We should. Nothing matters, he doesn't matter, you don't matter... the only thing that matters is this jungle, our home. And if it's under threat, we should unite and help it get back. And we will. Right?"

Jumbo wiped his tears and nodded weakly, though his heart still ached. "Yes," he said, his voice barely audible.

After a long pause, they fell into an uneasy quiet, the jungle around them still and silent. Then, suddenly, they heard it again—the unmistakable sound of footsteps, as if someone, or something, was following them. The tension in the air thickened, and their hearts skipped a beat.

"Hey, wasn't it Echo and her family we heard last time?" Max asked, his voice tense with worry.

Before anyone could respond, the question was answered in a way they never expected. Without warning, Prime-9, the monstrous chemically engineered bear, along with a group of men, lunged toward them from the shadows. The force of his arrival sent a wave of panic through the group.

The bear was enormous, towering over them, his muscles rippling as he roared with a terrifying, guttural sound that seemed to shake the very earth beneath their feet. His teeth gleamed like daggers, and his claws scraped the ground with each step, leaving deep marks in the dirt. The sight of him was enough to freeze them in place.

The three friends could barely move, overwhelmed by the sheer terror of facing such a beast. Slowly, Prime-9 advanced, pushing the three of them back, step by step. The humans were close behind, waving sticks, drums, and cans, making an awful, screeching noise that rattled their nerves even further.

Max, Rex, and Jumbo backed away in fear, their hearts pounding, eyes darting between the bear and the approaching humans. They had nowhere to go, trapped in the middle of the jungle with no chance of escape.

With a sudden, primal roar, Prime-9 charged, his movements quick and vicious. Max and Rex, their survival instincts kicking in, turned and bolted into the forest. They ran with all their might, desperate to escape the bear's wrath. But the humans were not far behind, still making noise and drawing closer to Jumbo.

Little Jumbo, terrified and confused, ran for his life, his small yet large feet pounding against the earth. His heart raced as the humans closed in on him, taunting and shouting. He had no idea where to go or how to escape. Fear surged through him, paralyzing him as he stumbled, trying desperately to outrun the danger.

And then it happened. After running for a distance, the ground beneath him gave way, and with a sudden crash, Jumbo fell into a small pit. His legs kicked helplessly as he struggled to climb out, but the sides were too steep. Panic gripped him as he realized he was trapped. He trumpeted loudly, his voice echoing through the jungle in desperation, but no one came. The humans, surrounding the pit now, laughed cruelly at his misfortune, the noise from their drums and cans ringing in his ears.

Jumbo's heart sank as the humans closed in, their mocking laughter echoing in the air. The more he tried to climb out, the more hopeless it seemed. Every attempt only caused him to slip further down. He trumpeted again, but it was in vain. No one was there to help. Only the cruel sound of the humans' laughter filled the jungle, drowning out his cries.

The scene was suffocating, the air thick with the stench of fear and helplessness. The pit felt deeper than ever, and Jumbo's strength was failing. He had nowhere to turn, no escape. The jungle, once his sanctuary, now seemed like a cruel prison. And the humans, so heartless in their pursuit, showed no sign of mercy.

"Hey don't cry, you idiot!" said one of the humans.

"We don't see you as a threat you fool! We need you when we rule this jungle, as our slaves." Their laughter echoed once again.

"Look at his eyes. Full of fear," another one said. "We need to see this fear all the time. You shouldn't forget this, tell your family about what happened to you today. Tell them we are coming for you, tell them we are going to make you guys our slaves." The human's voice rang out again, cold and devoid of sympathy.

Others laughed and continued the noise. The devilish laughter and sound echoed all over the jungle.

Meanwhile, Rex and Max were in serious trouble. The only thing working in their favour was their speed, which, compared to the massive Prime 9, gave them a slight edge. The beast's heavy footsteps rumbled behind them, but its size slowed it down. Max's heart pounded in his chest as they ran, each step heavier than the last.

Max, breathless and desperate, glanced at Rex. "Rex... Is he still behind us?"

Rex didn't answer immediately. "I..... don't.... want to ... look, ... please," he said, his voice strained with fear.

"Please, Rex, just look back!" Max urged.

Rex finally turned his head, still running. "We're safe... for now."

But the moment felt strange to Max, as if the world around him was suddenly moving in slow motion. Time itself seemed to stretch out, amplifying his fear, and in that eerie stillness, Max saw the trap ahead. His heart skipped a beat as the realization hit him.

"Rex! Watch out!!" Max shouted, but it felt as if his words were moving through molasses, the urgency hanging in the air like a heavy fog.

Rex, focused on the path ahead, didn't hear him in time. His foot landed on a hidden log, and suddenly, everything changed. Max's heart dropped as Rex slipped, his body lurching forward in a painful, helpless motion. He fell with a sickening thud, and in that moment, everything around Max seemed to freeze.

"Nooooo!!" Max screamed in horror as he watched Rex crash forward, his body twisting unnaturally as his head collided with the rope trap set just ahead.

The rope snapped tight around Rex's neck, jerking him into the air. Max's blood ran cold as he saw his friend's body hang suspended, helpless, his legs kicking weakly against the air. The world around Max seemed to slow to a crawl, each moment dragging out painfully.

Rex gasped for breath, his hands desperately trying to pry the rope away from his neck, but it was too tight. The knot had caught too quickly, and Rex was trapped, struggling but unable to escape.

Max's chest tightened as he stood frozen, paralyzed with helplessness. But as he looked up, the horror only deepened. Around them, Max saw several other animals—familiar faces—hanging upside down from the trees, their legs bound tightly in rope, suspended in the air. None of them were hanging by their necks, but their faces twisted in agony, legs flailing uselessly, each struggling to break free from their restraints.

But Rex... Rex was different. His neck was caught in the trap. His head hung limply, his body swaying slightly in the air, as his legs kicked feebly, a desperate attempt to break free. The other animals' struggles seemed distant in comparison to Rex's frantic movements.

Max's mind couldn't process it. This—this was his friend, his brother in this fight. Rex had been trapped by the very thing meant to break them, and it was happening too fast. Max couldn't do anything.

"Rex!" Max screamed, his voice raw with agony. He ran toward his friend, but it felt like the ground had turned to quicksand beneath him. His legs refused to move as fast as his heart demanded.

Rex's struggles were weakening. The desperation in his movements slowed, his body slumping slightly as the rope squeezed tighter around his neck. Max felt each moment like an eternity, helpless and paralyzed by the sight of his best friend fighting for his life and losing.

There was nothing he could do. Max screamed again, his voice breaking, but no one came. The jungle seemed to close in on him, suffocating him with its silence.

Rex's eyes fluttered. He tried to breathe, but the air was choking out of him. Max reached out in vain, but it was too late. The fight was leaving Rex's body.

Max watched, heart torn in two, as Rex's body went still, his legs hanging motionless now. His arms were limp at his sides, and his face was pale. Max stood there, frozen, as the life drained from his friend, unable to save him, unable to do anything but watch as his brother in this war died in front of him.

And then, in a moment that felt like an eternity, the world around Max seemed to crash back into focus. The jungle was no longer silent. The noises of the world, the rustling leaves, the distant calls of animals—everything came rushing back, but all Max could hear was the crushing silence in his own chest.

Rex was gone. His friend—his family—was gone. And Max, paralyzed with grief, was left alone, with only the echoes of his friend's final moments hanging in the air. The trap had taken him. The jungle had taken him. And Max could do nothing but stand there, broken and lost in the agony of what had just happened.

Roaring back, Prime 9 lunged towards Max with terrifying force. The ground shook beneath him as the massive creature charged, its claws swiping through the air. Max's heart pounded in his chest as the weight of the situation sank in. His mind, still reeling from the horrific sight of Rex's lifeless body, barely registered the danger as it closed in. He had to escape. He had no choice.

Somehow, he managed to escape the immediate danger. The further he ran, the more he heard the growls of Prime 9 fading into the distance. Max's chest heaved as he finally came to a stop, his body trembling with adrenaline and fear. He managed to survive."

"Maybe it was an accident," Arvind continues, his voice trembling slightly as he speaks, the weight of the memory pressing down on him. "If Max hadn't told Rex to look back, maybe Rex would have seen the danger in front of him. Maybe, just maybe, if Rex hadn't slipped, he would have only been caught by the trap with his legs tied, like the others. But there are no 'maybes,' no 'ifs' in this story. The truth is—Rex is gone."

Arvind pauses, struggling to find the right words. The children sit still, their hearts heavy, sensing the pain in his voice.

"That night... that night felt like it would never end. It wasn't just a night of fear—it was a night of losing someone you loved. For Max and Jumbo, it was a nightmare they could never wake from. The horror of seeing Rex... of seeing him like that... it tore them apart."

"The pain, the guilt, the helplessness—it was unbearable. Max kept thinking, 'What if I hadn't told him to look back? What if I had just warned him sooner?' But the truth is, no matter how many times you ask 'what if,' the outcome doesn't change. Rex is gone. And that loss, that feeling of powerlessness, it's something they'll never forget."

The room falls silent. The children feel the weight of the words, the sorrow in the air thick and heavy.

Arvind's story is more than just a tale—it is a reminder of the fragility of life, and how quickly things can be taken away.

Chapter 5

"I love you 3000," Niraj says playfully, looking at Ishan, who is lying dramatically as "dead Rex."

Nirav, quickly realizing what Arvind has said earlier about avoiding Avengers references, intervenes. "Hey, stop it, you guys!" he says, a bit embarrassed. "We're fine, Dad."

Priya cannot hold back her laughter. "Arvind, continue the story. Don't take breaks; it's spoiling the flow!"

Arvind, surprised by the encouragement, grins. "Well, well. First time my wife actually likes my storytelling," he says with a chuckle.

"Pappa, continue!" Ishan eagerly urges.

Arvind nods with a smile and picks up from where he has left off, diving back into the story.

"The tragic demise of Rex cast a deep sorrow over the forest, leaving all its creatures in mourning. Max was in deep depression; he couldn't face anyone. The thought of being the reason for his friend's death haunted him. Max refrained from attending Rex's funeral because of this. Rex had been a famous animal, known to many, and the funeral was a sorrowful sight to behold. The entire 14-member wolf pack was present. Lady Lion came alone without her pride, Jumbo and his family arrived, and Echo, the deer, and her family returned for the final time to see her friend.

In the funeral ceremony, Drake, the dominant male father of Rex, Luna, Rex's mother, and his uncle stood before the gathered animals. With a heavy heart, Rex's uncle decided to address the gathered creatures. His voice quivered as he began to speak.

"My dear friends, family, and fellow creatures of the forest, today we gather to say goodbye to Rex—the heart and soul of this land. From the youngest to the oldest, we all knew his name. His cleverness, his courage, and his spirit were known far beyond our woods. He always wanted us all to stand together.

But today, as we mourn his untimely departure, I must thank each and every one of you who has come to honour him. Your presence here is a testament to the love we all shared for him. Rex may have been a wolf, but he brought us all together in ways words can't describe. He had a gift—the gift of making the impossible seem possible, of turning even the darkest of days into something brighter."

He paused, choking on his words, before continuing.

"He died fighting for his friends. We warned him several times not to interfere, but.... fate..." He paused again, gathering himself before continuing. "Rex was taken from us far too soon, but his spirit will never fade. It will live on in every rustle of the leaves, in every whisper of the wind. And though we will miss him deeply, I want to say one thing: we must finish what he started." His voice broke, but he somehow regained his composure.

After a pause, he continued, his voice thick with emotion, "Thank you, Rex, for everything you were. You will forever remain in our hearts." His words broke, and tears welled up in his eyes. He stepped aside, allowing Drake and Luna to speak.

Luna, Rex's mother, stood motionless, her eyes locked in the distance. She seemed lost in her thoughts, perhaps reflecting on the warning she had given when Zara first went missing. She had always cautioned against the dangers ahead, but now, she found herself facing the worst of them—losing her son.

At a distance, Luna noticed Thorne, the old bear, standing alone. It was a rare sight, especially at a public gathering like this. He usually kept to the shadows, but today he was here—an unlikely presence among the crowd.

Without saying a word, Drake and Luna left the gathering. A complete silence descended on the crowd, heavier than any spoken words. The forest seemed to hold its breath. Slowly, the animals began to disperse, each step slower than the last, their spirits weighed down by the loss of one of their own.

"The situation is bad," said Lady Lion to Leo, the King, after returning from Rex's funeral. Max was sitting nearby, his eyes swollen from crying. Leo sat at the top of the summit as usual, with Rook, the eagle, beside him.

"And why did you go there?" Leo asked.

"Just think," Lady Lion replied, "if the same thing happened to one of our children, I can't even imagine it."

"You didn't answer my question," said Leo.

Lady Lion's voice grew more intense. "Oh really? You want to know why I went there? Because that's what rulers do—they address the issue, stand with them. And do you know how Rex died? Max and Rex went to investigate human activity, according to your orders. The trap was meant for Max, you know that? And Rex was doing all this for our son, to find

Zara. And you really want to know why I went there?" Her voice was filled with anger.

"I've already made my decision," the King said sharply, his voice holding a hint of frustration. "This is our family matter," the King repeated his decision. "I ordered Max to go. Rex being a part of this—was never my choice. Did I say Rex should go?" he asked, his gaze shifting between Lady Lion and Max, his eyes hardening as he awaited a response.

Max suddenly interrupted. "This is your family matter?" His voice cracked with emotion. "And you're still singing the same song? For your family matter, my friend died? For your family matter, Jumbo was trapped in a pit—traumatized, harassed, and left? Is it? For your family matter, many animals have been bound and tortured all over our jungle? They're threatening us, Dad, not just you! All of us, the whole jungle! Understand that!" Max shouted, his anger rising.

"Max, don't speak to your father like that," Lady Lion scolded him.

"Yes, I will speak! If it's the adults who need questioning, then it will be questioned. How can he think like this? I should've spoken up sooner. If I had, maybe I wouldn't have lost my friend. I don't know if my brother is even alive. I don't know the condition of Jumbo. Echo and her family left the jungle. And for the King, it's still just a family matter!" His eyes were red with rage.

Lady Lion remained silent, and so did Leo. Rook, the eagle, listened carefully, but did not intervene.

"I've heard the stories about the wildfire years ago, when your father was the King. He brought everyone together, fought together, and helped each other. We survived that fire when no one believed we could. And I've come to realize that it wasn't a mystery—it was unity. The united strength of all the animals saved us then," Max spoke again, his voice quieter now.

Leo listened carefully.

"We need to gather everyone, Dad. This is not just a family matter; this is a matter of our forest, our existence. We need them. We need to fight back against the humans. Zara is in danger. Our forest is in danger. The King must rise to the occasion, or the death of Rex will be for nothing." Max's voice broke as he cried.

Leo stood near his son, his arms tightening around Max, the weight of the situation settling heavily on his shoulders. The anger, the pain, the loss—it all came rushing in, and for a moment, he simply held his son, his mind racing. Lady Lion stepped forward, her eyes filled with grief, and joined the embrace. She leaned her head on Max's, her tears falling freely now.

For a long, quiet moment, there was nothing but the sounds of the forest around them, the crackling leaves and the gentle rustle of wind. Max's shoulders trembled, his emotions raw and unfiltered, and Leo felt them too—felt them as if they were his own. He had failed, not just as a king, but as a father.

He pulled away slowly and, without a word, turned to look at Rook. The weight of Max's words, the anger in his son's voice, now sank into his very being. His chest felt tight. The words that Max had said earlier rang in his ears, "*This is not a family matter. This is the matter of our forest. Our existence.*" Leo had known, deep down, that Max was right. But it had taken the rawness of the moment for him to truly understand.

He nodded to Rook, his gaze heavy with the realization of how badly he had misjudged things. Rook, always the one who saw the bigger picture, understood immediately. He moved without hesitation, beginning to plan a gathering—a public meeting that would bring together every creature in the forest.

As Rook made his way to organize the meeting, Leo stood frozen for a moment, his heart torn. He had been a king, but now, he had to be something more: a leader who listened.

Turning back to Max, Leo's voice was thick, as if struggling to push past the emotion, "I see it now, Max. You were right." He swallowed, looking at his son, his eyes filled with an understanding that hadn't been there before. "This isn't just about our family. It's about all of us. I... I will do better." His voice broke slightly, and for the first time, the great king allowed himself to show his vulnerability.

Lady Lion, who had been silent, placed a paw on Max's shoulder, looking up at Leo with a soft gaze. Her eyes were filled with pride, but also with the pain of a mother's loss. Leo turned to her and nodded slightly, acknowledging her strength and the weight of the shared grief.

Max looked up at his father, his anger still there, but softened now by the words of understanding. He wasn't alone in this anymore. The realization was a small, fragile comfort, but it was something.

"Thank you," Max said, his voice quieter now. He didn't need the grand gestures, but it was the first time he felt like his father was truly listening.

Leo hugged him again, this time with a newfound sense of connection. They stood together in the stillness of the jungle, both knowing that a change had begun. A change not just for their family, but for the whole forest.

A similar conversation unfolded in every family. The young animals of each family spoke to the older ones, urging them to understand the power of unity. They reminded them that this was not a matter of any one family's concerns, but a fight for all. And with that realization, a new resolve began to grow within the jungle, one that would bind them all together in their struggle for survival.

After many years, a rare and historic gathering took place. Under the silver glow of the moon, animals from every corner of the jungle began their journey toward the King's meeting. The night was thick with anticipation, and the air shimmered with magic. It was as if the jungle itself held its breath, knowing that this night would be one for the ages.

Families, who lived their lives in solitude, now walked side by side, their paws, hooves, and claws stirring the earth as they made their way to the heart of the forest. Each step felt like a ripple through time, watching the reunion unfold. Lions, elephants, wolves, monkeys, and birds, all mingled together in a unity that had long been forgotten. The very air seemed to shimmer with magic, as the path they walked echoed the footsteps of ancestors who had once gathered in this very place. It was a sight that Rex would have been overjoyed to see—perhaps, somewhere in the heavens, he would be watching over them.

As they gathered, the stars above twinkled brighter, and the moon bathed the jungle in a soft, ethereal glow. Nature seemed to recognize the significance of this gathering, and the animals walked in silence toward the heart of the forest, waiting at the base of the summit, eagerly to hear their king.

Max stood with the crowd, Lady Lion behind the King. As the King ascended the summit, he paused, his commanding presence filling the space.

The King addressed the gathered animals, with the historic openings like all the other kings in that jungle.

"Citizens of the kingdom, great and small. "

He took a pause and then continued, “I have seen a scene like this before, when I was a child. Long ago, I stood beside my father, Lothar, in this very place. His legendary speech that day still echoes in my heart..." Leo's voice faltered for a moment, as memories rushed back, heavy with their weight. "But I am not Lothar. I am not the leader he was. What he had—his power, his wisdom—carried us through some of our darkest times."

A long pause settled over the gathering, the weight of his words hanging in the air. It felt as if the entire jungle was holding its breath, waiting for what would come next.

"I thought the recent incidents that happened in the jungle, starting with my Zara's kidnap, was a family matter, but I see now that it is about more than just us," Leo continued, his voice growing firmer, though still laced with the hum of realization. "I have no shame in admitting my mistakes. I was corrected by my wife, and my son Max." His eyes softened as he looked at Max, who stood humbly in the crowd, a quiet pride gleaming in his father's gaze. "Today, I make some decisions, decisions that may change our future."

The crowd stirred in anticipation. King Leo took a deep breath, steadying himself for what he knew would change everything. He stepped aside, signalling the next part of his speech, and called, "My friends, step forward."

From the crowd emerged two figures—Drake, the formidable male wolf, and Sila, the commanding matriarch of the elephants. Their presence alone struck the onlookers, for never before had two species stood so boldly in unity. They climbed the steps to the summit, where Leo stood waiting. The sight was awe-inspiring, a symbol of something unspoken but deeply felt. It was unprecedented. No king had ever allowed another species to stand beside them at such a height. The moment was daring, surprising, and, in its quiet intensity, thrilling.

King Leo turned his gaze back toward Max, still standing in the crowd. Their eyes met—no words were needed. Max gave a brief nod, his silent acknowledgment of his father's decision. The King returned the nod, a smile flickering on his lips. In that brief exchange, a quiet understanding passed between them—a bond forged not just by blood, but by respect, humility, and the realization that the kingdom was ready for something new.

Sila stepped forward, her eyes filled with both sorrow and resolve. A hush fell over the gathering as every creature in the kingdom turned their attention to her. She spoke with a calm authority, her voice carrying across the crowd.

"We are hurt, wounded, and have lost some," she began, her words resonating with the weight of truth. "Yes, I said we—because this is no longer a matter of individual families. It is the matter of all of us, together. All the heads of our families, including myself, were too hesitant to act before, and that indecision has only made things worse."

She paused, taking a breath, her eyes scanning the sea of animals. The gravity of her words hung in the air, palpable, as every creature felt the sting of her confession.

"It is our young ones who had the courage to step forward and correct us," Sila continued, her voice softer now, but filled with emotion. "I'm a mother. I know how deep the pain runs in every mother's heart, in every family who's lost someone. And now... now we will give answers to every question the humans have asked. We will return their cruelty tenfold."

She sighed heavily, the weight of the future pressing upon her.

"Lions have been our kings for ages—strong and powerful," she acknowledged with a respectful nod toward the regal figures standing nearby. "We, the elephants, are also mighty in our own right. But let me tell you this: when it comes to leadership, when it comes to building a united front, the wolf is the ultimate leader. There is no doubt in my mind."

Her eyes turned to Drake, and the silence of the moment seemed to deepen as she spoke the next words with a sense of finality and anticipation. "So now, I ask Drake to step forward and take the lead."

The entire gathering leaned in, waiting with bated breath, eager for what was to come next. The King nodded, as Drake, the dominant male wolf, moved forward. The jungle held its breath, knowing that when Drake spoke, it was never just words—it was a declaration of action. His eyes burned with determination as he began, his voice low but steady, commanding the attention of every creature present.

"My fellow beings, great and small, of this vast and beautiful kingdom," Drake's voice reverberated through the crowd, commanding their attention. "We stand here today at the edge of history, in the darkest hour our jungle has ever known. This day, I promise you, will be remembered. It will be written into the very soil beneath our paws, because we have never faced a threat like this before."

He paused, letting the weight of his words sink in. His gaze swept over the crowd, and the pain and anger that burned in every animal's eyes were unmistakable.

"We have lost our beloved," he continued, his voice trembling with grief. "I lost my Rex. Zara is in danger. Jumbo has been humiliated. Our bodies have been broken, many of us tortured to death. The humans have struck us in ways we never thought possible, but we will not be defeated. We are stronger than they ever imagined."

Drake's voice grew louder, fiercer, as his heart spoke through every word.

"It's easy to kill humans—they are weak. They walk on two legs, they cannot run, they cannot fly, they cannot survive in the wild as we can. We are built for this. We are built to endure. And I swear to you, my brothers and sisters, the sun will shine on us again. The jungle will heal, and we will stand victorious."

He took a step forward, eyes blazing with determination, his words now laced with raw emotion.

"We fight not just for survival, but for the very soul of our jungle. We fight for our families, for our future. And we fight for the memory of those we've lost!"

The jungle seemed to pulse with the energy of his declaration. Every animal—no matter how small—felt the power of his words. There was a fire in their hearts, and it spread like wildfire through the crowd.

"We will fight! We will fight for our existence! We will fight for our jungle!" he roared, his voice shaking the very trees around them.

The sound of his declaration was met with a thunderous roar of unity, the ground trembling beneath their feet as the animals' voices rose together in a single, indomitable cry.

"FOR OUR EXISTENCE!" they shouted, their cries filled with defiance, courage, and an unbreakable bond.

The air hummed with energy, the jungle itself alive with the collective heartbeat of a kingdom united. They knew this wasn't just any fight—it was the fight for everything they had ever known, and they would not back down. The legend of this night would be passed down for generations.

Drake's eyes found Luna, Rex's mother, in the crowd. Her gaze locked with his, and in that instant, they shared an unspoken understanding—a vow. With tears in her eyes, Luna shouted, her voice breaking through the silence: "FOR REX!"

The words echoed through the jungle, and the animals, one by one, joined her. "FOR REX!!"

Max, watching this moment unfold with pride in his heart, understood that this day—this declaration—would be remembered for ages. He shouted alongside them, his voice ringing with emotion: "FOR REX!!"

The jungle knew, deep in its heart, that this was the beginning of something monumental. A war had begun, but they would fight with pride, knowing their unity could never be broken. Every creature understood the cost: a war where some might never return. Yet, they would die with pride, for their jungle and their families," Aravind reflects.

"I'm sorry, Dad," Nirav suddenly says, breaking the silence

"What?" Arvind asks, looking at him curiously.

Nirav jumps up from the bed, his face lighting up with excitement.

"AVENGERSS!" Nirav shouts, his voice full of energy.

The other kids, catching his excitement, immediately sprang to their feet, standing alongside Nirav.

"Assemble!" Nirav whispers in a low, determined voice, just like Captain America in Endgame.

Then, they all begin to run, their voices echoing with the same unity and strength they have just heard about in the animals' meeting, as they reflect on the intense decision to fight together, just like the Avengers in the movie.

Watching the children, the parents cannot help but laugh."Oh God, these kids!" Priya chuckles, watching them run off.

Chapter 6

"At the darkest hour of the jungle, the news of the gathering—an alliance of united animals—had already reached the human camps. They scrambled to prepare, convinced they had days, maybe even weeks, before the animals would strike. But they couldn't have been more wrong. The true danger wasn't ahead of them—it was already closing in from behind. The animals knew the forest like the back of their paws. Silent, swift, and with a deadly understanding of every shadow, they were already among them.

In the dense forest, a group of men made their way toward the watch hut they'd built atop a towering tree. The path ahead was barely visible, but they knew it well, the ground soft beneath their boots and the thick air making each breath feel heavy. They clutched drums, sticks, water bottles, and fruit in their hands. The jungle, once a familiar friend, now seemed to press in around them, its stillness unnerving.

"Actually, I'm scared to be out now at this time," one man admitted, his voice barely a whisper. His fingers tightened around the handle of his drum as if it could offer him some comfort. "I should admit it. I don't know how they'll respond. What have we been taught? Animals aren't predictable. "

The others fell silent for a moment, the only sound being the faint rustle of leaves in the breeze. It was the kind of silence that made every tiny sound feel amplified—each crack of a twig, each movement in the shadows could mean something. The man who spoke shifted his weight, clearly uneasy.

"Don't be a coward," another man shot back, his voice sharp, perhaps too sharp. "If they're unpredictable, so are we. They don't know what we're up to." He gave a nervous laugh, trying to ease the tension, but it sounded hollow in the air.

The wind shifted suddenly, and with it, the jungle seemed to stir. The men glanced around uneasily. The trees seemed to loom larger, the shadows deeper, as if the forest itself was holding its breath.

Then, in the distance, they heard it—the haunting, mournful howls of wolves that cut through the silence like a blade slicing through the air.

"Hey, did you hear that?" one man asked, his voice tight, his gaze darting nervously through the trees as if expecting the wolves to appear at any moment.

"Remember what Robert said? If we hear wolf howls, they're passing signals," another man recalled, his voice laced with fear. "We're done for."

A tense silence hung in the air, the distant howls of the wolves growing louder.

"What do we do if they attack?" one of them whispered, his eyes wide with terror.

"They won't. We're not alone," came a voice from the back, attempting to sound calm but cracking with uncertainty. "The wolves won't attack us. They know that."

"Right, and where were you when Robert said that part?" a third man mocked, his voice dripping with sarcasm. "If we're in a group, they won't attack. You remember that part, don't you?"

The mockery didn't ease the tension—it only thickened it, leaving the men looking at each other in a mix of doubt and fear.

"Okay, wolves may not come. But what if elephants do?" one voice asked, eyes wide with fear, his words barely audible in the dense, oppressive air of the jungle.

He laughed. "What's there to worry about? I'm an athlete. I've run long marathons. I've never heard of elephants running marathons," he chuckled again. "If they come, we'll do to them what we did to that elephant the other day. In fact, I don't think they'll even show up—after hearing what we did to him, they'll stay far away."

They laughed, their nerves easing for a moment. But then, one of them froze, eyes wide as he stared between the trees.

"Look! I saw something between the trees."

"What? Where?" they all turned, but saw nothing.

"I swear I saw eyes staring at me. Yellowish-red eyes. "

"Eyes? Yellow? Or red?" another man stammered, his face pale.

"Yellow... no, no, red!" The first man panicked.

They stared into the darkness, seeing nothing.

"Here, drink some water," one man offered, trying to calm the shaken one.

The night was thick with the chill of winter, the wind rustling through the bare trees like a whisper. Suddenly, a sound shattered the stillness—wild, haunting, and echoing across the valley. The wolves were howling again. Their cries, sharp and mournful, filled the air, a primal call that seemed to stir the very soul of the forest. As the eerie chorus reverberated through the darkness, a wave of tension washed over them, tightening the air with an unspoken dread.

"Look there!" the panicked man screamed again, pointing into the trees.

This time, the others saw them. Yellowish-red eyes gleamed from the darkness. The forest was alive with silent predators closing in on them.

"What's that?" one asked, his voice trembling.

"Elephant," another whispered in terror.

From the shadows, the massive matriarch elephant, Sila, emerged, her towering figure bathed in moonlight. Her eyes burned with fierce, ancient wisdom.

She stepped forward, and beside her, Jumbo, her young son, stood strong. They looked at the humans, their presence a reminder of the might of the jungle.

"Why aren't you using your drums? Come on, make some noise!" Sila's voice thundered through the night. "Why are your new friends so frightened, Jumbo?" she asked, turning to her son.

Jumbo smiled, his eyes gleaming with a new light. The soft, fearful gaze from the other day had transformed into a fierce, defiant glow. His once trembling posture had shifted; now, standing tall beside his mother, he radiated strength and confidence. His body language no longer expressed the helplessness he'd felt when the humans had tormented him. Instead, his stance was firm, his eyes filled with the fire of vengeance and the security of knowing he wasn't alone.

The humans froze, rooted in fear.

Sila trumpeted, her voice sharp. "Let's make a deal," she said, her tone cold. "You can run and save your life. After all, you're athletes, right? We're big, but we can't run long distances, can we? Fair deal, don't you think?"

The humans hesitated, standing frozen, unsure of what to do. They had no plan. Fear gripped them, paralyzing them into inaction.

"Run!" Sila roared, her voice echoing through the night.

The humans stumbled backwards in terror, confusion mounting. They turned to flee, their hearts pounding with panic.

But they didn't realize they were already surrounded.

Jumbo laughed. "Have you ever seen a stampede?" he shouted at them.

The humans didn't answer—they were too busy fleeing for their lives.

Jumbo's voice boomed. "Then let's show them!" He gave the command, and the elephants, hidden in the shadows, charged forward. The stampede erupted in a storm of rage, a brutal revenge for the torment Jumbo had endured. The elephants charged forward with terrifying force, their mighty bodies crushing everything in their path. The humans had no chance. Chaos unfolded as the herd surged through them, their trumpets echoing through the night. The ground trembled under the weight of the elephants, and trees were snapped like twigs as the humans were trampled, crushed beneath the sheer power of the stampede.

The humans screamed, but their voices were drowned out by the thunderous roar of the elephants. One by one, they were swept aside, their bodies left in the wake of the herd's fury. The stampede left destruction in its path, leaving only silence behind.

But one man, 'the marathon runner', managed to escape. He ran, his heart pounding in his chest, convinced he had outrun the stampede. For miles, he pushed forward, his legs burning, his breath ragged. He thought he had escaped, but exhaustion eventually overwhelmed him. He collapsed to the ground, unable to move another step, only to realize that he managed to escape only because he was spared by elephants, as Sila had commanded earlier— "Leave that marathon runner for me alone." And now, in the stillness of the night, he realized too late that the true danger had always been closer than he thought.

At the very moment—he was at the feet of Sila.

In a frantic attempt to rise, he stumbled, but his strength had abandoned him. His legs were too weak, his body too broken from the terror and exhaustion. He couldn't lift himself off the ground. His arms trembled, but the strength to push himself up was gone. He struggled, gasping for breath, but it was futile.

As he lay there, defeated, his vision blurred, and the cold ground pressed into his bones. He tried to rise but failed. His legs wouldn't cooperate. He was too weak to escape.

Sila's voice was calm, but her words cut like ice. "I just want to correct you on one thing," she said as she loomed over him. "Just because you haven't seen us run long distances doesn't mean we can't. And if we decide to kill one... no 'marathon runner' can ever outrun us. Understood?"

As she said this, she walked through him, stepping over him as though nothing had happened. So calm, so cool. For him, it happened all of a sudden. He was already drained from the run, his body on the brink of collapse, but now he couldn't even scream. It was as though the very first step Sila took upon him shattered his bones, a crushing force beyond comprehension. He could do nothing but lie there, paralyzed, as the life drained out of him.

The forest fell quiet, the tension dissipating as the echoes of the stampede faded into the distance. Sila and the herd turned away, but there was no triumph in their stride, no sense of finality. They knew their part was not yet completed.

For Sila, it had never been about revenge; it was about protection—about what any mother would do when her child was in danger. The torment Jumbo had endured at the hands of those humans had been unbearable. She had given them back what they had taken from him. Every thunderous step of the stampede was an act of retribution, a declaration that no harm would befall her young again. It was not mere vengeance; it was the fierce, unyielding love of a mother defending her child.

The night deepened, its silence pressing in like a thick blanket, broken only by the distant whispers of wind rustling through the trees. The moon hung low, casting its silver glow across the darkened landscape. Shadows stretched and shifted, long and eerie, as if the night itself were watching, waiting.

At the edge of a quiet lake, the stillness was pierced by the sound of soft paws against the earth. Drake, the dominant wolf, moved toward the water, his fur ruffling slightly in the cold breeze. He stopped at the water's edge, looking out into the vast dark. The world seemed suspended in time.

As he bent down to drink, his sharp eyes caught a flicker in the shadows—just a movement, too swift to be certain. His ears twitched, and a sudden chill ran down his spine. But when he glanced back, the night seemed undisturbed. Shrugging off the unsettling sensation, he continued drinking, the cool water refreshing his dry throat.

Then, without warning, the air seemed to shift. The shadows darkened, and Drake's fur stood on end. He slowly raised his head, eyes narrowing, and there—standing just beyond the water—was the towering figure of Prime-9. The engineered bear's massive form loomed, its presence swallowing the moonlight around it. The bear's dark eyes glinted, fixed on Drake with an eerie, unnerving focus. The night had gone from tranquil to heavy with the weight of danger, and the tension hung thick in the air.

The bear roared, its massive body lunging toward Drake with terrifying force. But Drake, swift as ever, darted aside, narrowly avoiding the crushing blow. The bear spun, its confusion palpable, its eyes scanning the shadows. But Drake was already gone, blending into the darkness, the only sound the fading echoes of his footsteps. The bear growled in frustration, its senses heightened, searching the night for its elusive prey.

The forest fell silent for a moment; the only sound was the bear's heavy breaths. Then, a wolf's howl pierced the air, sharp and haunting. The bear's head snapped toward the sound, and there, atop a nearby hill, stood Drake.

Furious and driven by instinct, the bear charged toward the hill. But by the time he reached it, Drake had vanished again. The howling continued, relentless, and the bear's mind, already frayed, began to crack. Now, the sound echoed from every direction, pulling him into deeper confusion. Each howl gnawed at his senses, disorienting him, and driving him into a state of mindless fury.

He ran for miles, each step guided by the howls, but they never led him to his prey. The sound seemed to come from all directions, disorienting him further. The bear could no longer distinguish between echoes and reality. The howls were driving him mad—ripping away any sense of control, pushing him deeper into a frenzied state. His chemically engineered mind, designed to be a killing machine but not equipped for complex thought, could not comprehend what was happening. He didn't feel, he didn't think—he only chased, driven by the sound.

Frustration and rage consumed him. He roared in madness, but the howls continued, just out of reach. His senses overloaded, his mind turned to pure chaos. The sound stopped abruptly, and for a moment, the silence was deafening. The bear, caught in his twisted state, moved slowly, cautiously, as if unsure of his surroundings.

He stepped into an open area, a greenish meadow, the night now thick with tension. And there, standing in the distance, was Luna—the mother wolf. Her eyes glowed red in the moonlight, sharp and unwavering. The howls returned, echoing in his ears, drowning him in their call.

Without thinking, without a second's hesitation, the bear charged at her, roaring in blind fury. His mind was clouded by the relentless sounds, his body moving purely on instinct, without the slightest regard for strategy or reason. Luna, the iron lady, stood motionless, her gaze steady and unmoving, watching the bear charge toward her.

Before the bear could reach her, the ground gave way beneath him. The bear fell into a carefully hidden pit trap, his enormous frame crashing into the depths. The howls, still ringing in his ears, finally ceased as the bear struggled in the pit, but it was too late. The bear, driven mad by the sounds, had been outwitted.

The bear's massive frame slammed into the pit, his bloodied body raking against the jagged edges as he struggled to rise. His vision blurred from the impact, and it took him a moment to regain his senses. When he finally looked up, the scene before him was one of pure terror, even for a creature as powerful as he.

At the rim of the pit stood a circle of wolves—Drake, Luna, and the entire pack. Their eyes glinted in the moonlight, silent, deadly. Behind them stood Sila, the matriarch elephant, and her troop, towering and unmoving. Large rocks, poised above, were ready to drop at a moment's notice. The bear's eyes widened in understanding—it was over.

The real truth hit him then. Drake hadn't been the prey. He was the bait. The bear had been lured into this trap with the howls, manipulated into a maddened state by the relentless noise, chasing phantoms until he was too far gone to think. His pursuit had led him here, straight into the hands of the wolves and the elephants.

Drake's calm eyes met his for a brief moment, and the bear realized it had all been orchestrated. The whole chase, the howls that had twisted his mind, the endless running—it had all been a part of the plan. It had never been a mistake for Drake to come to the lake. The bear had been played.

Panic surged through his mind as the full weight of the situation settled in. The wolves stood ready, the elephants silent and looming, and there was nowhere to run. With his body broken and trapped, surrounded by enemies, the bear understood that his fate had already been sealed.

Sila's deep voice echoed through the night, filled with a raw, primal power. "For the existence!" she bellowed, and the first rock tumbled down into the pit, crashing with earth-shaking force. It was followed by another, then another, until the pit was filled with a deadly barrage of rocks, each one bringing the crushing weight of finality.

The sound of rocks falling grew louder, but amidst it all, Luna's quiet voice broke through, trembling but fierce. "For REX..." she whispered, her words carrying the weight of a mother's grief and resolve. With that, she pushed the final rock into the pit, sealing Prime-9's fate. His twisted body lay crushed beneath the rubble, and the death of the engineered bear was complete.

Luna collapsed to her knees, overcome by grief. Her body trembled with the weight of the loss, and tears welled in her eyes. Drake, ever the silent protector, approached her. His presence was calm and steady, offering the only comfort he could. The entire wolf pack stood behind her, their hearts heavy with sorrow. They had avenged their fallen, but the cost of that victory was not lost on them.

As Luna's cries filled the air, probably for the first time after the demise of Rex, Sila approached, her massive form stepping closer. She knelt beside Luna, her wise eyes softening with understanding. For a long moment, there was silence—just the quiet sobs of a mother who had lost her child, and the unspoken bond between two mothers who had fought for their children.

Sila gently pressed her trunk against Luna's side, offering her silent support. Their shared grief and their shared strength united them in that moment. The wolves and elephants stood together, a legendary scene of mothers coming together to protect and avenge their children, to heal the wounds of the past, and to honour the lost.

The giant bear lay defeated, its massive body crushed beneath the weight of rocks, a symbol of the battle fought and won. It had been the humans' most fearsome weapon, but now, it was no more. The forest seemed to breathe a collective sigh of relief, but the victory was fleeting, for the true danger had not yet passed.

As the wolves and elephants stood in solemn unity, Rook, the eagle, soared down from the sky. His wings beat the air with a silent urgency, his keen eyes scanning the ground below. He landed with a soft rustle, his presence commanding attention.

"Humans down, bear down," Jumbo said, his voice steady as he updated Rook on the situation. He met Rook's gaze, his eyes narrowing slightly. "And what about Vexor, the tiger, and Robert—the main man?" Jumbo asked.

Rook replied, "Vexor is dealt with—killed by King and Max."

Everyone exchanged smiles, relief washing over their faces. The threat of the tiger was no more.

But Drake, sensing something was amiss, asked, "But why aren't you happy?"

Rook looked down, his eyes shadowed with concern. "King and Max have been captured by Robert and some of his men."

"What?" Sila's voice held a note of shock, her posture stiffening as she processed the news.

Drake's brows furrowed. "How many men left now?"

Rook glanced around, his voice heavy. "Only a few. But they have King, Max, and Zara, and they're planning to escape with them. We need to act fast."

Drake, Sila, and Luna exchanged glances, the weight of the situation settling in. The battle wasn't over—not yet.

Outside the human camp, three guards stood weak and battered, their bodies covered in blood from the intense fight. With sticks in their hands and guns slung over their shoulders, they appeared more like shadows of their former selves, barely able to keep watch. Vexor, the tiger, lay lifeless in the dirt, his once formidable body soaked in blood, a casualty of the battle.

Inside the camp, King, Max, and Zara were held captive, each trapped in a cage. King and Max were both injured, their wounds bleeding freely as they sat slumped against the bars, their strength ebbing away. Zara, too, was exhausted, unable to muster the strength to move, his body spent from the ordeal.

Meanwhile, Robert rushed about, packing his things in a frantic hurry. His own wounds added urgency to his movements as he prepared for the escape. Despite the pain, he pressed on, knowing that time was running out.

"I'm taking you guys with me," Robert said coldly. "Don't ever think I'm going back because I'm afraid. I'm going back to come back stronger. When I return, I'll have you all with me. Just like I brought Prime-9, I'll have you chemically engineered, made unemotional, and trained to fight by my side."

King roared in defiance, thrashing against the cage in an attempt to break free. But it was useless—the cage held firm and his efforts were in vain.

Robert laughed cruelly. "The king," he said mockingly, shaking his head with amusement.

Suddenly, the air was pierced by the sounds of gunshots, followed by the frantic screaming and crying of humans. Robert's face turned pale as panic gripped him. He grabbed his gun, his fingers trembling, and hurriedly made his way toward the door of the camp.

The cries seemed to fade for a moment, the eerie silence hanging in the air. Robert strained his ears, trying to catch any sound from the outside, but all he could hear was the pounding of his own heart.

With caution, he stepped out of the camp, holding his gun tightly, scanning the surroundings. But before he could take another step, a powerful force kicked him back into the camp, sending him crashing to the ground.

Dazed and shaken, Robert struggled to regain his footing, his eyes wide with terror. He couldn't comprehend what was happening.

The camp was eerily quiet for a moment, and then, a deep, thunderous roar shattered the silence. It was a sound that shook the very earth beneath their feet. Zara, despite her fatigue, straightened up, eyes wide with disbelief. The roar carried a fury and power she had never felt before. Max and King, too, felt the weight of the sound, their eyes darting to the entrance of the camp.

From the shadows, with a thundering roar, Thorne emerged.

The old bear, bloodied and furious, stormed into the camp with a force that made the ground tremble beneath his massive paws. His fur was matted with blood, dripping from his claws and maw. His eyes burned with rage, a fire that had been fueled by years of pain, loss, and torment. The strength of his roar was felt in every bone, every corner of the camp.

Zara couldn't believe what she was seeing. Despite her exhaustion, the sight of Thorne's return filled her with a strange surge of energy. Max and King, too, stared, wide-eyed, as the once-dominant figure of the forest made his way into the camp, like a force of nature.

Robert, who had been preparing for his escape, froze in terror as he turned and saw Thorne advancing. The bear's eyes were locked onto him, filled with a primal fury. Thorne moved like a shadow of vengeance, his steps thunderous, his body a symbol of unstoppable wrath.

Before Robert could even react, Thorne reached him in a flash. With a powerful swipe of his massive paw, he sent Robert flying, the human crashing into a far corner of the camp with an agonizing thud. The bear's roar echoed through the camp, sending chills down everyone's spine as he stood over Robert, growling in triumph.

"Yes, the mistake is with me," Thorne shouted, his voice echoing through the camp, filled with ancient fury. "I should have spared your grandfather when he and his men first tried to set this forest on fire. So that your whole community remembers what happened that night! I still remember the fear in your grandfather's eyes—the terror of facing something far greater than his weapons."

Robert froze, his body shaking with disbelief. He had never heard this version of the infamous old firebreak. The truth was more horrifying than he could have imagined. Thorne was not just a bear; he was the enchanted guardian of the forest, a creature of old magic, bound to protect this land from any who would harm it.

Suddenly, there was a loud creaking sound, the metal cage doors slowly groaning open, almost as if by some unseen force. The three lions inside—King, Max, and Zara—stared in shock as they realized the cage had opened on its own. It wasn't the work of any human or animal. The magic of the forest was at play.

Robert's eyes darted from the open cage to Thorne, his mind racing. He couldn't understand. How had this happened? The cage was locked, secured with the power of man—yet now, it was undone, just as the bear had broken free from his own chains in the past.

"They are my children!" Thorne roared, his voice shaking the ground beneath them. "This is my home! I am the beast who guards this land. I killed your grandfather and his troop when they tried to destroy it with their flames, and I will protect it for as long as I draw breath."

Thorne's enormous form loomed over Robert, his eyes burning with the weight of centuries of fury. He reached out with his massive paw, gripping Robert by the collar and lifting him off the ground. Robert's heart pounded in terror, but there was nothing he could do as Thorne brought him close to the walls of the camp.

"Don't dare come back," Thorne said firmly, his voice calm but filled with authority. "I'm not making the same mistake I made all those years ago. I spare you now, but remember this: tell your people that this land is protected. Here lies a magical bear, as old as the forest itself. If you ever return, you'll face me."

With that, Thorne gave Robert a final warning, raking his claws lightly across his face, leaving a lasting mark. "Carry this with you, and tell your people to stay away."

"Run for your life," Thorne added, his voice softer but still heavy with the weight of his words. "Or stay, and die here."

King, Max, Thorne, and Zara slowly made their way out of the camp, with Thorne carefully carrying Zara in his strong arms. As they left, a strange calm spread over the camp—fire began to spread on its own, the flames burning brightly, as if the jungle itself had taken control.

The jungle seemed to welcome them back, its creatures stirring in the shadows. The forest, once again, stood strong and united, a place of peace."

Arvind sighs, taking a long pause before continuing, "The jungle stood eternal, its heart forged by the sacrifices of those who fought for its freedom. Mothers, warriors, and friends had united, their spirits forever bound to the enchanted land they had protected. With each sacrifice, the forest grew stronger—forever free, forever enchanted."

He leans back, a sense of relief washing over him as he finishes the tale. Thinking that this story will live on, passed down like the echoes of the forest—its memory carried through the winds, whispered by the trees and remembered by his children.

"Yeeee," Ishan, Nirav, Niraj, and Priya clap their hands. Arya is also smiling.

"Great story, Dad," Ishan says.

For a moment, the room is filled with a warm silence, the kind that only comes after a tale well told. The kids exchange looks, processing the story's deeper meaning, their faces thoughtful.

Arvind watches them, a quiet pride in his eyes, before breaking the silence. "What did you understand?"

The kids look at each other, then answer, "Unity is the key to success."

"And?" Arvind asks.

"And?" The kids look confused.

Arvind's smile softens, his voice warm with wisdom as he speaks. "Remember always the sacrifice of a mother. She will give everything she has, just to ensure the safety and well-being of what she has birthed."

The kids grow emotional, hugging Priya and apologizing for the chaos they have caused earlier that night. Priya hasn't expected the story—or the moral of it—to take such a turn. She is taken aback by how Arvind has turned everything around. Still, she hugs the kids back warmly, her heart softening as she looks at Arvind, a mix of surprise and admiration in her eyes.

"I said right, I'll fix this," Arvind says softly. They smile at each other. It seems that, in the end, Arvind has not only shared a story, but also stitched their hearts back together.

"Okay, it's already 3 am. Let's sleep. Come, come," Priya says softly, trying to gently usher everyone to rest.

"Can we sleep here all together tonight?" Niraj asks, his voice tinged with innocence and hope.

Priya smiles but shakes her head. "There's not enough space, dear," she replies, glancing around at the cozy, slightly cramped living room.

Nirav, eager to stay close, speaks up. "No issue, we can adjust." He shifts to make space on the floor, his tone casual but warm.

The parents exchange glances, both silently agreeing that a little discomfort is worth the togetherness.

"Alright, I guess just this once," Arvind says with a chuckle, and Priya nods.

Lights off.

As the kids drift off to sleep, Priya turns to Arvind and asks, "Arvind? Are you asleep?"

"No, tell me," he replies.

"Do you think the kids really understand the true essence and relevance of your story at this age?"Priya asks.

Arvind thinks for a moment before replying, "They might not understand it today, but I'm sure they'll remember this whole day, this whole story. And maybe, at some age, when they recollect this day, they'll truly understand what the story meant."

Priya smiles and hugs him.

And with that, Arvind and his pack fall asleep peacefully.